COME
ON
IN

15
STORIES
ABOUT
IMMIGRATION
AND
FINDING
HOME

Edited by
Adi
Alsaid

COME ON IN

15 STORIES ABOUT IMMIGRATION AND FINDING HOME

inkyard PRESS

ISBN-13: 978-1-335-14649-6

Recycling programs for this product may not exist in your area.

Come On In
Copyright © 2020 by Adi Alsaid

All the Colors of Goodbye
Copyright © 2020 by Nafiza Azad

The Wedding
Copyright © 2020 by Sara Farizan

Where I'm From
Copyright © 2020 by Misa Sugiura

Salvation and the Sea
Copyright © 2020 by Lilliam Rivera

Volviéndome
Copyright © 2020 by Alaya Dawn Johnson

The Trip
Copyright © 2020 by Sona Charaipotra

The Curandera and the Alchemist
Copyright © 2020 by Maria E. Andreu

A Bigger Tent
Copyright © 2020 by Maurene Goo

First Words
Copyright © 2020 by Varsha Bajaj

Family

Everything
Copyright © 2020 by Yamile Saied Méndez

This edition published by arrangement with Harlequin Books S.A.

For questions and comments about the quality of this book, please contact us at CustomerService@Harlequin.com.

Inkyard Press
22 Adelaide St. West, 40th Floor
Toronto, Ontario M5H 4E3, Canada
www.InkyardPress.com

Printed in U.S.A.

Contents

They came in by the dozens
Walking or crawling
Some were bright-eyed,
some were dead on their feet
And they came from Zimbabwe,
or from soviet Georgia
East Saint Louis, or from Paris,
or they lived across the street
But they came, and when they
finally made it here
It was the least that we could do
to make our welcome clear

—"Color in Your Cheeks,"
the Mountain Goats

● ● ●

ALL THE COLORS OF GOODBYE
Nafiza Azad

● ● ●

To Ishraaz, the brother I left behind.
I love you.

I say goodbye to the hibiscus first.

I planted them with my amma on my seventh birthday. Three red hibiscus plants, two orange, four pink, and one yellow. They have been my responsibility ever since. I water them, I count the buds and wait for them to bloom. Once they do, I tell the flowers my secrets and all the prickles in my heart.

Now I have to leave, and I don't know who will look after them when I am gone.

• • •

This morning my abbu returned with a thick brown envelope from the post office in town. When he opened it, his eyes widened first with disbelief and then with joy. He told us we are leaving. That we are moving to another country. He said that home will be a different shape, color, and feeling from now on. Why would the idea of leaving make him so happy?

• • •

A grove of mango trees grows by the road just a little distance from our house. This grove is filled with large boulders and smaller stones that my grandfather placed between the roots of the trees. When the wind rushes through this grove, it sings a strange, mournful tune. I say goodbye to the song and to the stones.

• • •

Five months ago, there was a military coup in the capital city. The prime minister, in the midst of celebrating his first year in office with chai and cookies, was deposed, and someone called George Speight announced himself captain. The radio shot bulletins into the air. The media, international and local, went into a frenzy. Some people looted the capital city. Others augured the coming of The End. We, on the other side of the island, some three hundred kilometers from the capital city, found ourselves on a break from school. Suddenly Fiji was no longer safe.

Even though nothing has changed on our side of the island, even though there has been no violence or looting here, people insist that things are no longer the same. They talk about the government and its supposed bias toward the natives of our country. They say that it is time to leave. My father cloaks his eagerness to be away and calls it a concern for my future. My mother is silent—as she always is—in front of my father. I do not want a future if it dawns in a place I do not know, but no one listens to me.

My cousins and I, drunk on the sunshine and the sugarcane, can't see what the trouble is. Our lives were unaffected by the coup, by the political riots, by everything outside our village—until my father brought home the brown envelope that will change everything.

● ● ●

My room is not very big. The bed, leaning against one wall, faces the door while the other two walls have screened and louvered windows that somehow provide no barrier to the mosquitoes. The faded curtains wage daily war with the unrelenting sun that makes the obnoxiously blue carpet on the floor even brighter. The walls are a gentle pink. Tube lights overhead provide light and death to moths. My broken-down wardrobe is beside the door. My precious cosmetics (if you must know, one tube of half-used pink lipstick, a tube of lip gloss, baby powder, and a comb) lie on what serves as a vanity table. The mirror is not attached, and I often think it is going to complete its slide onto the floor and lose the little lease it has on life. My shalwar kameez have the place of honor and hang from hangers, flaunting their grace and their glory. In a little green tub I keep under my bed are all the clothes I wear at home. I have a bookshelf crammed with secondhand books, books borrowed, and books received as gifts. The walls contain posters of Bollywood actors I might have crushes on. The back of the door is decorated with lipstick kisses. This room has held all my corners and filled me with myself. It grew as I did and blooms as I do. When the setting sun paints the walls orange and shadows emerge from under the bed to hide the damp on my cheeks, I whisper a goodbye to my room.

● ● ●

I have an older brother I don't really know how to talk to. I also have six first cousins I grew up with. Their parents live in two different wings of my grandmother's house, which is two hundred meters away from mine. Three cousins per family, four girls and two boys. Our names rhyme and our thoughts are collective. We have fought each other and fought for each other. We have whispered secrets about our changing bodies, assuring ourselves that we are normal. We know each other like other people know themselves. The spaces between us are thick with memories.

Two hours after I found out, I tell my cousins about the brown paper envelope, about my father's words, about leaving. They are quiet. We sit on the cool rocks under the mango trees in the grove my grandfather built. The wind makes music out of the day. Perhaps they, like me, cannot understand what leaving means. Perhaps, they cannot comprehend, either, the nature of distance and what it will do to us. I don't know how to be myself without them. Do they know how to be themselves without me?

My eldest cousin is angry. "Do you know how big your goodbye is?" She spits out the question. Pauses. Then answers it herself. "It is the size of forever."

"Then I won't say goodbye," I reply stubbornly. It is not as if I am leaving because I want to.

"Some goodbyes do not need to be spoken," she replies.

"You will come back, won't you?" my youngest cousin asks anxiously. She's only seven. There are ten years between us.

Even if I do come back, the home right now and the people right now will no longer be as they are. As I change, so will they and so will this place. When I leave, I will lose this place and these people. I will lose myself. Who will I be without the mountains, the mango trees, and the hibiscus around me? I do not want to know.

• • •

At the bottom of the garden in front of my house is a field. In the far-right corner of this field are a breadfruit tree, a well, a saijan bhaji tree, and my mother's precious collection of chilli plants. When the chillies are ripe, every breath feels like a storm. My grandmother and I harvest the chillies because, for some reason, she and I are not affected by the heat that makes everyone else cry. Our fingers pluck the red, yellow, orange, and green fruit without burning for days afterwards. I stand in that green corner that is bordered on two sides by sugarcane fields and smell the deep brown of the soil in which the chilli plants grow. The water in the well reflects the afternoon sky. I pick a ripe breadfruit hanging heavily on the branch and leave my goodbye stamped on the soft bark of the saijan tree.

• • •

Our family of four sits around cups of chai during teatime. The silence is full of the things we don't know how to say to each other. The afternoon outside tempts with its golden light and a breeze that will make silk of your hair. I can feel my father's gaze on me like little weights on my skin but I am too busy looking at my brother, memorizing him, learning all of him in the smile he no longer smiles and the sadness that has found a recent home in his star-bright eyes.

You see, the people who decide who gets to go say he is too old to be considered a dependent of the family, as if age determines the bond a person has with their relatives. The government of this new country we are moving to won't let him come with us, so my parents decided that he is old enough to be left alone. I wonder what conversation my parents had with my brother. I wonder what words they used to let him know that we are leaving. That he is not coming with us. I asked my father why we are going if my brother can't come with us. My father had no answer, so he told me not to be impertinent.

● ● ●

Our days have become finite. The sun rises daily anyway. Except for one day when it rains. I seize the chance and say goodbye to the silver raindrops dancing on the ground under the mango trees. For a while, I try to dance along with them, but their grace pronounces my lack of it so I stop and let the warm rain wash me through. Perhaps I cry, but the rain keeps its secrets.

Because it is raining, the blue mountains on the horizon gain waterfalls. I sit on a rock under a tree and squint into the distance. When I was younger, I wished to climb these mountains and see the waterfalls. Perhaps I will someday. Probably I won't. Just in case the future isn't kind, I say goodbye to the mountains and their waterfalls too.

● ● ●

My ammi gives me a suitcase and tells me to start packing. I have to fit seventeen years of my life into one suitcase. I stare at her, but she won't look at me. She won't listen to me. No one will.

I don't have many things, but they are still too many for this one suitcase. What do I leave behind and what do I take with me? I am being told to divide myself into pieces and choose which parts of me are the most important. My heart will remain behind. It has told me its decision, and I cannot convince it otherwise. I will leave, a hollow version of myself.

The walls of the place I call my own are now a collection of empty spaces where things used to be. Shelves have been emptied and closets are now a spectacle of hangers and little else. All rooms except the one used by my brother are affected by our upcoming excision from this land.

I drift in the empty spaces like a ghost-to-be, learning how to haunt a house. A house that will now belong to my brother. A house in exchange for a family. I wonder if my brother feels like the trade is worth it.

● ● ●

One crisp dusk when the skies are a red befitting my mood, I say goodbye to the azaan that comes from the east where the masjid is. After night eases into all corners previously owned by light, the people at the mandir start their puja. The music of the sitar and the accompanying voices raised in prayer fill the air. I stand outside in the garden, alone for once, and the frogs skirt the area I stand in as if they too know the state of my heart. I look up at the sky. I don't have a camera to capture the heavens heavy with stars, so I look my fill and try to impress the image into my heart. I know there will be other skies and other stars, but nothing will ever compare to these.

● ● ●

Even though I am still here, close enough to touch, a new distance breathes itself into existence between me and my cousins. They do things without including me. They share secrets without telling me. I have been pushed out even though

I am still here. Even when I am still a branch of the tree. They have cut me off and set me free, even though I don't want to be cut off or free.

• • •

The night before we leave, we are invited for dinner at my grandmother's house. My aunts, uncles, cousins, and grand-parents are all there. Our neighbors are there. Everyone from the village is there. First, second, and third cousins are there. The adults talk about our good fortune and how we are lucky to be leaving. They wish us happiness and pray for our health in the new country that belongs even less to us than this one does. My great-grandparents were brought to this country, and they chose to stay here. They clung to this land, mixing their blood and their sweat with the soil, wanting to belong to it and wanting it to belong to them.

I sit ensconced among my cousins, turbulent and stormy. I am one gale away from being a hurricane, but my eldest cousin has her arm around me. She squeezes my shoulders and reminds me to be respectful in front of people who have sheltered us at our worst and held us up at our best.

• • •

I spend the night with my cousins. The adults leave us alone. The mosquito netting around the bed gleams ghostly in the dark. An hour after midnight, my cousins and I slip out of the room in which we are to sleep and onto the ve-randa wrapped around the house. We can hear the beat of the lali, urgent in the thin night air, coming from the di-rection of the Fijian koro. My second-eldest cousin lights a candle and sets it on the floor. We sit around it, a circle of island witches, browned limbs and bright eyes. No one speaks for a moment, but I feel their gazes on me. The purpose for which we are gathered thrums unspoken between us. They are readying themselves to finish saying the goodbye that sits warm on all our tongues.

My youngest cousin cries, gasping sobs that rise in the honey-eyed air of the hot night. My eyes sting in response, and I bite my lip. Our faces are illuminated by the flickering flame of the candle. My eldest cousin whispers a story then, about the time we were chased by angry hornets. Someone speaks about the time we were almost carried away by the sudden flood that made a river out of a drain. A guffaw suddenly breaks loose, and we are a cacophony, caught somewhere between laughter and tears. This is their goodbye to me. I will myself to remember each detail of this last night.

• • •

The next morning, I skip breakfast to visit my house one last time. I touch the green cement walls and kiss the hibiscus plants. I plant a tear in the soil and hope it grows up to be a wish that will bring me back.

• • •

On the way to the airport, I say goodbye to the road. I am not reconciled to the idea of leaving. I cannot separate myself from these islands, but my cheeks are wet and taste of salt. The salty sea that surrounds these islands is retreating from me.

• • •

At the airport, I say a farewell to my uncles and aunts whose homes have been my own ever since I learned the meaning of family. Their faces, their smiles, their smells, and their stories are home. I hug my cousins extra hard.

My brother, I save for last.

I stand in front of him and hold on tight to his hand. Seven years stretch between us. Our conversations have been awkward and uncomfortable, as if we don't speak each other's language, but there are times when we don't need language to speak. I remember the times his warm back comforted me when I most needed it. I remember his weird snorting laughter when I told a joke no one else would laugh at. I remember fighting over the last fry in the box. I remember him singing me to sleep once.

I have been trying to learn the planes of his face, afraid that I will forget it and him. Afraid that I will forget the scent of him that I define as brother: the smell of sunshine, sea, and a sweetness I haven't been able to find elsewhere.

I have been running away from this moment, but time has caught me in its grasp and refuses to let go until I live through it.

You see, I have been haphazardly saying goodbye to everything—even to the stones in the backyards—but only at this moment do I realize the immensity of goodbye. Only at this moment do I realize the brutality of it. What is goodbye? Does it mean *I will see you again*? Or perhaps *I love you*? Or perhaps it means *hold on to me and don't let me go, because I am not certain I will be myself anywhere but here*. I don't know. I haven't lived long enough or experienced enough to have the answers.

My father says we need to go, but I cling to my brother harder, scared because the hurt in my chest is far more severe than anything I have felt before. Perhaps this is the prelude to some kind of death I do not yet have the language to articulate. My brother puts his arms around me and hugs me back as I cry. I cry as I have never cried before. I cry as I never will again.

Finally, even though I am not ready, my brother pulls away. He tries to wipe my tears but more keep falling. He attempts a smile and fails. His eyes are wet too.

"I will look after your flowers," he says. "Your hibiscus flowers. I will take care of them."

I blink hard and nod. "I will come back," I promise. I might not be the same person when I do, and my family will change with time, but one thing will always remain the same no matter what: This place is, and always will be, home.

"We will be waiting," he says, and lets go.

AUTHOR'S NOTE

Dear Reader,

My parents and I moved to Canada from Fiji in August 2001. I was seventeen years old and not at all willing to leave behind my entire life and everyone I knew. In Fiji, we lived on a sugarcane farm in a small village called Vitogo. In "All the Colors of Goodbye," I give you a fictionalized version of what my goodbyes looked like.

ABOUT THE AUTHOR

NAFIZA AZAD is a self-identified island girl. She has hurricanes in her blood and dreams of a time she can exist solely on mangoes and pineapple. Born in Lautoka, Fiji, she currently resides in BC, Canada, where she reads too many books, watches too many Kdramas and writes stories about girls taking over the world. Her debut YA fantasy, *The Candle and the Flame*, was released by Scholastic in 2019.

•••

THE WEDDING
Sara Farizan

•••

"**Y**ou look wonderful, Darya," Mom said as she pushed back my shoulders so that I would stand up straight. She was always lecturing me about my posture and how important it was that I carry myself like a lady. For the sake of the family and the photos that would be taken of us, I was wearing a dress to my cousin Shayla's wedding. I still hadn't quite figured out how to be comfortable with, as my mom would say, my "burgeoning womanhood." I felt like a neon-pink sausage, waddling around in high heels that squeezed my feet. I could feel a blister forming on my pinkie toe already.

"I still can't believe you're wearing this," my sister Tara said, pointing her phone in my direction. I didn't smile for the photo, but she was grinning from ear to ear. Tara liked to glam up, put on makeup, wear dresses, and today she'd gone all the way with a lavender dress and popping bright-red lipstick. She looked good. She did it for herself and not for anyone else's approval, but it wasn't really my bag nor did I think it ever would be.

"If you put that online, I will never forgive you," I said through gritted teeth. The most I did in the grooming department was tweeze my eyebrows, and even that could be dangerous. Sometimes they were uneven or too thin, as I never knew when to stop plucking. Lately, I'd let them grow and do their own thing.

"Look at my beautiful daughters," Dad said, approaching us in the hotel lobby. He was in good spirits but had dark circles under his eyes. He'd done most of the driving from Boston to Montreal the day before, and we'd arrived later than the GPS had said we would. So far, Montreal felt like Europe and North America had gotten together and had a baby that wore a lot of denim and liked hockey. This was, of course, a generalization as I'd been in the country for less than twenty-four hours, but most people at the hotel had been very friendly and polite, so that stereotype about Canadians seemed to hold up.

Dr. Hamid Sadeghi, my grandfather, stood beside my dad, a little shorter and more fragile than his son, whom he once towered over. My grandfather looked handsome in a navy blue suit. His eyes were wide, and he reminded me of a kid who was about to meet Mickey Mouse at Disney World.

"Darya," Grandfather said. "You look…"

"Better than usual. I know." I was dressed like this at the sofreh aghd, the wedding ceremony, but I guess my being gussied up was still a shock to my family. What did I normally look like, to warrant this kind of enthusiasm? I mean, I usually wore jeans and a T-shirt, but it wasn't like I dressed only in burlap sacks or anything.

"No. You don't look happy," he said. "You don't have to wear that if you don't want to."

I loved him so much I thought my heart might burst.

"She can't show up to the reception in a T-shirt. What would everyone say?" Mom was fussing with a blow-dried piece of my hair that was out of place. She'd spent most of the morning tugging at my hair with a flat iron to make sure I was as presentable as possible. My hair was thick and curly, which might look good on other people, but I always forgot to use the fancy leave-in conditioner Mom bought me. My hair without conditioner gave me a Cousin Itt from the Addams family quality. It was yet another way I managed to disappoint her.

"Yes, we wouldn't want the Iowans and Iranians we'll probably hardly ever see again to start talking about Darya's fashion choices," Tara muttered. "How will we sleep at night?"

"Don't be fresh," Mom said to Tara. She let go of my hair and looked at me like I was a Wendy's Spicy Chicken Sandwich when she had ordered coq au vin from a fancy French restaurant. Not what she'd had in mind, but satisfactory. "Shall we go?"

Tara, Mom, and Dad walked ahead to find the ballroom. I trailed behind with Grandfather and held his hand.

"When did you grow up?" Grandfather asked me.

"I didn't. It's these shoes," I replied.

"It's not the shoes," he said. "Your older sister always talks back to your mother. But you don't. You're sophisticated."

I laughed a little. *Sophisticated* wasn't a word I would associate with myself, considering Cap'n Crunch Berries was my breakfast of choice and I still wore Batgirl pajama bottoms to bed. "Are you excited?"

He nodded. "I want to make sure my brother and I have time together," he said. "He wasn't at the ceremony. I've talked to him on the phone, but the last time I went to visit him in Iran was so long ago. Maybe this is the last time we'll see each other. I don't know." That was the reason the bride and groom were having their wedding in Canada—so that my great-uncle and his wife could attend. Travel bans really put a damper on festive occasions. It was why I wasn't putting up a stink about what I was wearing. I squeezed his hand.

I wanted him to have all the time in the world.

A crowd of well-dressed wedding guests were mingling in front of a table outside the ballroom. I saw Dad hugging his sister, my aunt Mahnaz, who was wearing a maybe-not-super-age-appropriate red dress. I thought she wanted to make a big splash this weekend. She'd been waiting for her only daughter, Shayla, to get married for a long time. Aunt Mahnaz would complain to my dad on the phone about how worried she was that Shayla might be single forever, which to me hadn't sounded bad at all. Now that Shayla had finally found a husband, Aunt Mahnaz was going all the way with an extravagant wedding, no matter what country it had to be held in.

"Hello, Baba," Aunt Mahnaz said with absolute joy as she hugged my grandfather. When she let go of him, she noticed me, and her mouth opened in shock. When we'd visited each other on Thanksgivings over the years, I had always worn my typical attire of ill-fitting, punk rock wear. "Darya, you're so dressed up! I love it!"

I sensed a theme. Everyone preferred this fake version of me. Actual me wasn't enough. Lately I felt that way about everything that I was. I wasn't Persian enough (on Dad's side), I wasn't Turkish enough (on Mom's side), I wasn't feminine enough, I wasn't straight enough, I wasn't gay enough, and these days, I got the impression that my government was telling me I wasn't American enough. I was born and raised in the States, but I still got asked where I was from. I knew people didn't mean Massachusetts.

"Hi, Aunt Mahnaz," I said as I hugged her, letting go of whatever annoyance I felt at everyone who liked this hyperfeminized version of me. "Congratulations!"

"Thank you, Darya joon. I am so happy this day has come," she said. I'd never seen so many of Aunt Mahnaz's teeth at one time before.

"Is Majid here?" Grandfather asked with a slight crack in his voice. He looked around.

I'd met my great-uncle and his wife, Narges, once. They'd visited us five years ago in Boston after my grandmother passed away. I hated everything about that time, especially how ripped apart my grandfather had been. It was like he'd aged ten years overnight. But it would have been even worse if my great-uncle hadn't been able to come see my grandfather in his time of need. I didn't know much about the law, but I hoped someone who did would make sure the travel ban was temporary.

"They called from the airport," Aunt Mahnaz assured him while rubbing his shoulder. "Customs took a little longer than expected, but they will be here. Paul sent a driver to pick them up." Paul, Shayla's groom, hailed from Iowa. The two of them met in Washington, DC, where Shayla was a human rights attorney and Paul worked for a nonprofit focused on saving the environment. I thought they'd met through a dodgeball league for do-gooders or something.

"Good, good," Grandfather said before taking a deep breath. The only other time I'd seen him this on edge was at the hospital when we didn't know if Grandmother was okay or not.

"Come. I'll show you to our table," Aunt Mahnaz said, taking my grandfather by the arm and leading him into the ballroom. I joined my sister who was staring at the tiny placards on the table.

"Where are Mom and Dad sitting?" I asked her.

"They're at table two," Tara said as she picked up the placard with her name on it. "We're table eleven," she said as she found the card with my name on it and handed it to me. "You know what that means." She rolled her eyes. I think she assumed that, because she was eighteen, she wouldn't be assigned to the kids' table anymore.

To be honest, I dug a kids' table. There was always a chance you'd be served macaroni and cheese, plus no one wasted breath on small talk. Kids' table talk was very direct. Questions like, "How old are you?" and "Do you like dogs?" and my favorite, "How come your eyebrows are so thin/bushy?" depending on the day.

Tara slowed her pace, probably so that I could keep up with her in heels as we walked into the ballroom. The giant crystal chandelier overhead lit an empty wooden dance floor, tables with centerpieces made of white flowers, and a small bar with guests lined up to get a drink. Servers flitted from guest to guest, serving hors d'oeuvres to women in stunning dresses and men in tuxes, while the DJ played some jazz at a low volume.

We arrived at table eleven to find two young boys already seated. One looked about twelve and the other maybe six. They looked like they were related to one another and like they belonged to the groom's side of the family.

I sat down next to the six-year-old while Tara sat across

from the twelve-year-old, who blinked a lot when he saw Tara. I'd been told by my bandmates that Tara was super hot, which creeped me out, but I understood that this poor kid wasn't prepared for puberty to hit him all at once.

The six-year-old stared up at me. His nose was running, and he was wearing a red bow tie with suspenders. His round cheeks were begging to be pinched, but I hated when people did that to kids. Grown-ups should at least ask permission before they grabbed baby flesh.

"Are you here to marry Uncle Paul, too?" the little one said to me.

"No. He only gets to marry one person," I said. "I'm Darya."

"I'm Wyatt. I have a Spider-Man game on my mom's tablet. I can't play it now because it's dinnertime, but I can show it to you later and we can play."

"Wyatt, that's all I want to do. Ever." The kid and I were going to get along fine.

"You found a friend on your wavelength," Tara said, giving me a golf clap.

"Jealous?" I asked her. I think she was a little. Wyatt was adorable.

"That's my brother, Craig," Wyatt said, pointing to the boy who was mooning over my sister. "He's allergic to nuts so we can't have any peanut butter in the house. But that's okay because I love him."

"That's my sister, Tara," I said, nodding in her direction. "She's allergic to joy but Mom says that's because of something called hormones. I love her, too. Sometimes."

"You're hilarious," Tara muttered. "Maybe I will post that photo of you in a dress after all."

I glared at her. She laughed and took her phone out to take another photo of me.

"Hi," Craig said, introducing himself to my sister. "Uncle Paul said you're from Boston?"

"Yup," she said, looking at her phone and not giving him much to work with.

"That's cool. I guess you must be Patriots fans. I'm a Vikings guy. Well, not really. Football isn't my jam. I'm into basketball. Snowboarding, too. There must be great snowboarding and skiing near where you live because it's cold most of the time. We have that in common. Cold climates. Winter's my favorite season. Do you like winter?"

Tara smiled at her new admirer's rambling. "Winter's rad, Craig," she said with a charitable grin before she turned her attention back to her phone. Craig beamed, as his very white cheeks turned cherry red. Oh what power she wielded over the male species. I hoped she did some good and smashed the patriarchy with it.

Suddenly, we heard a jovial yell in Farsi. I turned to see my grandfather cradling his brother's head with reverence in his hands. Grandfather was smiling with tears running down his cheeks. The two men held each other, and everyone around them became very quiet, as if not wanting to interrupt the moment.

"Why are they crying?" Wyatt asked me.

"They're happy to see each other," I whispered to him.

"But they're crying. You cry when you're sad," he whispered back to me.

"They're a little sad too, I guess," I choked out, keeping my tears at bay. I was wearing mascara, a rare occurrence, and I didn't want to spend the rest of the wedding looking like a raccoon. My grandfather and my great-uncle backed away from each other a little, still holding on to one another's arms as they spoke in Farsi. Now they were smiling through the tears.

"How come?" Wyatt asked, leaning into me a little.

"Well, you know how you love your brother Craig?" Wyatt looked at his brother and nodded. "Imagine he lived somewhere very, very far away."

"Like in outer space? On Endor?" *Star Wars* fans start so young.

"Sure. Like he was hanging out with Ewoks on Endor and you were on Naboo."

"Can I be on Endor? That's more fun."

"Okay, you were on Endor and you couldn't visit your brother because you weren't allowed on his planet."

"Because of Darth Vader?"

I didn't feel equipped to explain a condensed history of foreign policy, world events, or unfettered xenophobia to a six-year-old. Maybe we'd see each other at another family function when he was older and we could discuss it further.

"Something like that," I said.

"Oh," Wyatt said quietly.

"But, you're here with your brother. My grandfather is here with his brother. And we're all here to celebrate your uncle Paul and my cousin Shayla. On the planet of Earth."

He considered this as he watched my grandfather greet his sister-in-law, Narges Khanoum. My parents walked over to them and they embraced one another.

"Okay," he said. The room became noisy again as people introduced themselves to one another and reconnected with old friends and relatives.

"I'm going to go say hello to them," I said to Wyatt. "Be right back, young padawan."

I walked over to my grandfather and his brother, Majid. Grandfather wiped at his eyes and smiled wide when he saw me.

"Darya! He made it," Grandfather said.

"Yes he did. Salaam Amu Majid," I said, putting my cheek to either side of my great-uncle's for the imaginary kiss greeting.

"Hello, Darya," Majid said with a thick accent. He and Grandfather then said what I'm pretty sure were complimentary things about me in Farsi. I recognized some words like *beautiful* and I smiled back. I understood some Farsi, but I couldn't speak much of it.

I couldn't be totally upset with my parents for not equipping me with secondary language skills. When I was seven, I had Farsi classes on Saturday mornings, and on Friday afternoons I had Turkish classes—to appease my grandparents on my mother's side who were from Istanbul—but neither my mom nor my dad spoke either language at home, and I got so busy with music lessons, it all sort of fell by the wayside.

Both my parents were born and raised in the States, so each could speak the respective language of their parents, with American accents, but when they got together, they spoke to each other in English. I took French at school, so I was more likely to be able to talk about the weather to someone in Paris than I would to someone in Istanbul or Tehran, and that made me feel slightly ashamed. Like I'd lost something.

"Your grandfather tells me you're an excellent musician," Majid said in Farsi. I blushed.

"I'm um...thank you," I said back in Farsi, but struggled with the words for *bass guitar* and *feminist punk/pop fusion band.* "I like it," was all I could manage.

Grandfather was beaming. I didn't think punk was his music genre of choice, but he came to every school talent show and had pitched my band for his hospital holiday party even though our songs were totally inappropriate for that sort of function. "Menstruation Frustration" was no "Frosty the Snowman."

The jazzy background music for cocktail hour suddenly stopped.

"If you could all please return to your tables, we're about to welcome the bride and groom," the DJ with the gelled faux-hawk announced into his microphone. I kissed my grandfather on the cheek before I toddled back to the kids' table.

I sat down next to Wyatt. A woman had brought him a plate of appetizers.

"Hi! I'm Mary. Paul's sister," the blonde forty-something said, reaching out her hand.

"Oh hi! It's great to meet you. I'm Darya," I replied. "Shayla's cousin."

"I hope my boys have been on their best behavior." Mary wiped the corner of Wyatt's mouth with a napkin. "They were so excited to sit with the teenagers!"

"We're fine, Mom!" Craig said, sitting up straight in his chair. His eyes were bugging out of his face, as if he were trying to telepathically communicate that she was free to go at any time. I think he was embarrassed, what with Tara seated across from him. Mary didn't seem to notice.

"Wyatt's my new best friend. If he wants to be?" I asked him.

"I already have a best friend. His name is Justin. He's six and a half. But you can be friends with us, too," Wyatt said. His nose was no longer running now that his mom had come to visit.

"I'm so happy to hear that you're getting along, since now we're family." Mary gave Wyatt a squeeze.

I supposed we were. Should Paul and Shayla have children, they'd probably look like a mix of Wyatt and me. What a pack of little heartbreakers those hypothetical kids would be.

A familiar instrumental came on loud and clear through the speakers, playing a traditional version of a song called "Mobarak Baad" that was played at Persian weddings. Tara and I grinned at each other. Aunt Mahnaz was going all the way.

"Ladies and gentlemen," the DJ announced. "Please welcome Mr. and Mrs. Becker-Ghorbani!"

Everyone cheered Paul and Shayla as they held hands and boogied onto the dance floor. I cheered for the hyphenated last name! Shayla's dad had passed away when she was in college, but I knew he would be thrilled that his name and legacy would continue.

Paul and Shayla let go of each other. Paul put his arms in the air and shimmied his shoulders like a Persian groom would. All the guests applauded wildly, especially my grandfather, who stood up at his table and began to dance in the same way. Shayla's simple white dress was cut in all the right places to make her look taller and elegant. She and Paul languidly moved their arms in the air as they danced with one another. Paul's hip-swaying action wasn't so bad, and clearly they'd practiced the dance. They didn't look alike, and maybe they didn't have a lot in common on paper, but when they danced, Paul and Shayla looked like they were always meant to be together. When I looked at Paul, I felt like he had always been at our family gatherings, even though they'd met only a few years ago. It was a good thing my grandfather had moved to the States, and that Paul's family had once moved to the States from Europe. I wondered how many people might not find the love of their lives because they were not allowed to live in certain countries. I didn't know if I'd have a special someone someday. Barf. Maybe they'd be from Endor.

Tara had her phone out recording the first dance. I knew my grandfather was going to watch it over and over again. He was a huge softie and had asked Tara to record as much of the wedding as she could.

When the song ended, a server brought a microphone to Paul. Everyone applauded their dance while the two caught their breaths and gazed at each other. Wyatt clapped and squealed next to me, as if excited to be able to make as much noise as possible at a grown-up party.

"Thank you," Paul said, holding Shayla's hand, waiting for the crowd to settle down. "Welcome and Khoshamadid." Paul pronounced the word for *welcome* in Farsi without difficulty. "Shayla and I wanted to begin by saying how grateful we are that you could come to one of the happiest days of our lives. We want to thank our family who traveled from Iowa, our family who traveled from DC, our family who traveled from Boston—" Tara yelped really loud after hearing our city shout-out "—and our family from Iran." He pronounced it E-rahn rather than I Ran. I loved this guy. "We wanted all of our family here, because you have supported us, you have loved us, you have given us the tools to be loving people, and no matter where you are in the world, no one can separate family. Especially a family who loves as much as we do."

This received a lot of cheers. What Paul was saying sounded nice, and I felt the love in the room, but families could be separated every day. Were being separated every day. Paul passed the microphone to Shayla.

"We especially want to thank Paul's parents, who are so lovely and who raised such a beautiful man," Shayla said. Paul blushed and gave an aww-shucks shrug. The guests laughed a little at that. "We want to thank my mother, who helped make this day happen and who shows Paul and I so much love every day. We want to thank Paul's sister, Mary, for all her help and kindness. And we want to thank my grandfather, Dr. Sadeghi, for making today possible by being the rock of our family."

Shayla then addressed my grandfather and the other guests from Iran in Farsi. I didn't understand all of it, but I watched my grandfather's eyes well up as Shayla said words I did understand, like *love* and *gratitude*. I hoped she mentioned that he'd been invited to the US over four decades ago and had forged a life for himself and his family. That he'd treated countless patients, saved the lives of people from all over the world who'd found themselves in Boston. That whether or not he was a physician, he was one of the most wonderful men in the world and we should all be so lucky to have him in our lives. I don't think she said all that, but it's what I wanted everyone in that room to know.

"Are you happy crying or sad crying?" Wyatt asked me.

"Both," I said, wiping my eyes. So my mascara might run. I could always freshen up my face in the bathroom.

• • •

After dinner was served, the DJ welcomed everyone to the dance floor by playing some surefire wedding hits by the likes of Kool & the Gang and the Bee Gees. Wyatt sat in Mary's lap, playing his Spider-Man game on an iPad.

Craig was on the dance floor trying his best to impress Tara with moves he no doubt would bestow upon the ladies at future middle school dances. He kept moving his shoulders up and down and leaning from side to side. Tara looked amused, giving him bits of attention during "Celebrate," but then turning to dance with Mom once a new song started.

Aunt Mahnaz was having a ball, stalking the wedded couple and making the photographer follow her around to document every moment of Shayla and Paul's happy union from various angles.

"I've never seen my brother so happy. Or dance so much," Mary said as she looked out on the dance floor.

"Same goes for my grandfather," I replied. He was snapping his fingers with his hands high in the air, his brother clapping alongside him as he swayed. It was special to see Grandfather look so…relaxed. Whenever we visited him at home, he would sometimes watch the news and get a look of worry. He wouldn't say anything, but I knew he was anxious about his family in Iran, about the sanctions, about the travel ban, about things he had no control over. He'd spent his entire life trying to help people, but there were some obstacles that seemed so insurmountable that it made me feel so small to think about them. Today, my grandfather looked at peace. It was a memory I'd never want to let go of.

"Little man, you want to dance?" Mary asked her son as she placed a hand on the edge of the iPad, signaling playtime was about to end.

"Okay." Wyatt let go of the game and scooted off of his mother's lap. "Can Darya come?"

"Why don't you ask her," Mary said sweetly.

"You wanna dance?" he asked me.

How could I say no to that face? "I'd love to," I said. He ran onto the dance floor, but my feet were killing me. I inched toward the floor but winced with every step.

Grandfather noticed and walked over to me. "Darya joon,

take off your shoes," he said as he gave me a kiss on my cheek. "I want to dance with the most beautiful girl in the room."

"Mom will be embarrassed if I go barefoot," I shouted over the music. I'd always tried my best to be the kind of daughter she wanted, like Tara, but it was getting more difficult the older I got.

"You could never embarrass anyone. Everyone should be so honored you decided to dance with them. Don't let anyone's ignorance make you feel that you don't belong somewhere. You belong wherever you are," he said in my ear. When he backed away from me, he held on to my shoulders and looked at me like I was the only person in the room, like he wanted me to believe that who I was, who I was growing up to be, was just fine. More than fine. I bit my lip and nodded. "Baba Karam," an old Persian song, started playing through the speakers. "Now we must dance!"

I held on to his arm as I lifted one foot up at a time and took off my shoes. I placed them under a table and joined him and the rest of my now larger family.

I didn't worry about what I looked like or that I didn't quite have the movements mastered. I didn't worry that Tara was going to record my awkward dancing. I didn't worry whether I was making a bad impression or about how I looked in this stupid dress. I didn't worry about what might come next for the world.

I was dancing with my grandfather. He loved me as I was, and that was more than enough. That was everything.

ABOUT THE AUTHOR

SARA FARIZAN is the critically acclaimed and award-winning author of the young adult novels *If You Could Be Mine, Tell Me Again How a Crush Should Feel*, and *Here to Stay*. Her short stories have been featured in the young adult anthologies *The Radical Element: Twelve Stories of Daredevils, Debutants, and Other Dauntless Girls, Fresh Ink, All Out*, and *Hungry Hearts*. She has an MFA in Creative Writing from Lesley University, lives in Massachusetts, kayaks way too much, and thanks you for reading her work. You can follow her on Instagram @sara.farizan.

WHERE I'M FROM
Misa Sugiura

RUDE

It's pouring rain the day I move into my dorm freshman year at Duke University. My parents and I walk down the hall, wiping rain off our faces and checking room numbers. 210… 212… 214. My roommate, Chloë, is already in the room with her parents.

Introductions and small talk ensue: what rotten luck we had with the weather today, of all days. What the flight was like from Minneapolis-St. Paul to Raleigh-Durham, where we stayed last night, how the rain caused three accidents on the highway between here and Chloë's hometown of Charlotte.

"So," say Chloë's parents to mine, "where are you from?"

"We live outside of Minneapolis," my father answers, looking confused—didn't we just go over this?

"Oh, yes, right. But where are you really from?"

"Mom," says Chloë quietly. She looks at me, clearly mortified.

"What?" says Chloë's mom.

But my dad doesn't notice, doesn't care, or maybe he doesn't want to embarrass Chloë's parents. So he tells them, "I was born and raised Takarazuka, Japan." He nods at my mom. "Natsume is from Ōsaka."

Later, as we say goodbye outside the dorm, I tell them that they don't have to humor anyone who asks them where they're really from. My mom says, "But we are really from Japan."

"Yeah, well, when I'm asked that question, I'm going to say, 'Minneapolis is where I'm really from,'" I say, but my mom shakes her head.

"Eriko, that's rude," she says. "Don't do that to people."

GUARDIAN ANGEL

When I was in eighth grade, a Japanese kid showed up at school. She was awkward and pimply, and on her first day she wore a sort of sailor uniform with a navy skirt and a white middy blouse with a big navy scarf tied in a bow. To top it off, her name was Miho, which is a pretty name in Japanese, but I just knew that the boys were all going to ask her, "Are you a ho? 'Cause that's what your name says."

Mrs. Mintz, our homeroom teacher, pulled me aside before class and introduced us, beaming. "Eriko, I'm appointing you to be Miho's guardian angel for a few weeks," she said, and she moved my seat partner and best friend Zayna so that Miho could sit next to me instead. "I know you'll help her get acclimated and make lots of friends."

How could I possibly help this girl? I didn't speak enough Japanese to be able to translate anything beyond the simplest conversational phrases. I was suffocating at the bottom of the dogpile that was the eighth-grade social hierarchy, struggling to hang on to my elementary school friends as they changed and clawed their way up and away from me.

Miho looked at me with dull eyes in a round face. She murmured, "Yoroshiku onegai shimasu,"—a phrase I vaguely understood to be a polite greeting of some kind—bobbed her head at me in a deferential little bow and came over to the desk next to mine. She did another head bob at me as she sat down. Now that she was next to me, I could see that she had probably been crying earlier. I felt sorry for her—how miserable it must feel to be new, to not speak a word of English, and to have to start off in that ridiculous outfit that I was sure her mom had made her wear, with that awful name, and she wasn't even pretty.

But I felt even sorrier for myself. Miho was exactly the kind of person that I feared everyone saw when they looked at me: weird, awkward, foreign. Japanese. I could not afford to take on an anchor like Miho, with her Japanese face and her Japanese clothes and that humiliating little Japanese bowing thing she kept doing every time I looked at her. I hadn't asked to be her friend, I told myself. It wasn't fair to lump me with her just because she came from the same country as my parents.

Eighth grade. Sink or swim. Eat or be eaten. I endured Miho's presence next to me in class, muttering a few broken Japanese sentences to her when I absolutely had to. Once the bell rang, I cast her off and went running to Zayna and Sophie.

"Oh, her?" I said. "She's Japanese, not like me. Real Japanese people are weird. Look at her. Look at how weird she is."

CHOPSTICKS, AGE 13

Zayna and Sophie and I spent the day at Schulze Lake Beach that weekend, and Sophie's mom got us Chinese takeout for dinner. I used chopsticks, they used forks.

"How do you *do* that?" they asked, not for the first time, and not for the last.

AMERICAN CITIZEN

The summer after Miho, we went to Japan and my mother enrolled me in a sleepaway camp so that I would learn to speak Japanese. I was surrounded by a hundred Mihos, girls who Mrs. Mintz had thought I would understand. No one was unkind to me, but they gasped when I poured soy sauce on my rice. They stared, shocked, when I sat crisscross (only boys do that!). The toilets were awful squat toilets.

One day, a girl asked me when I was going to come home to live in Japan. I explained that I was an American, so I'd probably stay in America.

"You're not American," she said.

"I am, too."

"You're Japanese."

"Yes, but I'm also American."

She gave me a long, hard look. She asked me gently, "Have you not seen yourself in a mirror?"

"I know my face is Japanese. But I am American because I was born in America." I didn't know how to say *birthright citizenship* in Japanese. Or in English, for that matter. All I could do was keep repeating, "I was born in America."

She shook her head. "Make sure you look in a mirror when you get home. You're definitely Japanese."

CHOPSTICKS, AGE 18

My roommate Chloë's mom visits Duke one weekend and takes us out for sushi.

She asks me, "Can you use chopsticks?"

DOUBLE

Shortly after that week of sleepaway camp in Japan, my mother and I passed a Starbucks on the way back from the train station to my grandmother's house in Osaka. It was a steam bath outside, and I was dying for a taste of home. I asked my mother to come to the counter with me to help me order, but she insisted I try ordering on my own first. "It's practically the same menu," she said. "Even the sizes."

So I walked up to the counter and ordered a grande Double Chocolate Chip Frappuccino. I said it slowly, so that the barista could understand me.

I got a blank stare in return.

"Grande," I said. I held my hands in the air, one over the other, grande-height apart. "Dou-ble. Choco-late chip. Frappu-cci-no." I pronounced everything carefully.

"Gu-rande," the barista repeated, and held up a grande-sized cup. "Fu-rap-pu-chiino?"

I nodded, encouraged. "Double chocolate chip."

Nothing.

"Double," I said slowly. I held up two fingers and said, "Ni," for good measure. Two isn't the quite same as double, but it seemed close enough.

Before I could continue, the barista furrowed her brow and reached tentatively for a second cup.

"No, no," I said. "Double. Dah-bu-ru."

She shook her head apologetically.

I looked desperately at my mother.

"It's not on the menu," she said.

"So? It's not on the menu at home, either."

"That's not the way it works here," she explained.

"Well, it should be. That's the way it works at home."

My mother shrugged. "You are not at home."

CHOPSTICKS, AGE 14

The day after the Starbucks incident, my mother's best friend from high school had us over for dinner at her house.

"Can you use chopsticks?" she asked me.

HISTORY

Mrs. Mintz paired us up to do presentations on different countries and their cultural contributions. Naturally I got paired with Miho, and we did Japan. It was okay, actually, because Japan is pretty great: castles. Samurai. Ukiyo-e. Taiko. Anime. Manga. Yuzuru Hanyū.

Miho wore a fancy kimono. We showed clips of *Sailor Moon*, handed out manjū, and passed around her collection of manga. Miho wrote everyone's names in katakana. People thought it was cool. I was proud of us both, and for once, I felt good about being Japanese. Miho smiled at me. I smiled back.

Then someone said, "My grandfather died in Pearl Harbor."

People looked at me and Miho. Miho looked at me.

I wanted to say, That wasn't me. That's not my country.

I wanted to say, What about Hiroshima? My great-aunt died in Hiroshima.

But the thing is, I'm not Japanese.

In the bathroom, I heard Sasha, the alpha girl of my class,

snicker and ask her friends if they'd seen the way all the nerds went apeshit over *Sailor Moon*.

The next day, Miho thought we were going to be friends, and she smiled at me again. This time I didn't smile back.

CHOPSTICKS, AGE 12

I wore them in my hair once, after seeing a picture of a fashion show online. Sophie and Zayna thought it was cool. My mother thought it was disgusting. "Would you wear a fork in your hair?" she said.

WE

I am home from college, and my dad takes me for burgers and shakes at the diner. While we eat, he asks why I supported a Native American protest of an oil pipeline being built near their land. "First of all, it's a threat to their supply of clean water. And second of all, it goes through land that's sacred to them. After we basically wiped them out and forced them to live on reservations, the least we can do is respect their wishes about something that affects their lives now."

"Why do you say 'we'?" my father asks. "Our family was still farming rice in Japan when that happened. And you're not even white."

"Because..." I have to think about that one for a moment. "Because it was America that did it. And I'm American."

"What do you say when you talk about Hiroshima, where Haruna-obasan died? Who is 'we' then?"

I don't have a good answer to that question.

"Do you say 'we' when you're talking about America today?"

"Well. Yeah."

"Even when the government does something you disagree

with? Like weak gun control or anti-immigrant laws? Still 'we'?"

"They."

My dad shakes his head. "English is hard."

I don't think it's just English that's hard.

FEAR

Three months after she arrived, Miho went back to Japan to live with her aunt. My mother blamed me.

"You were mean to her," she said.

"Mom. The girl was a freak. We had nothing in common. You expect me to give up all my friends to be friends with someone like that?"

"If people don't want to be your friend because you are Miho's friend, then they are not the real friend."

"They are real friends. She just didn't fit in."

I knew in my heart that my mother was right. I knew that I was being a coward. I knew that the right thing to do, the kind thing to do, would have been to be Miho's friend. But Miho and I being Japanese together would have doomed us both, and I was afraid of testing my friends, of not fitting in myself. My fear was greater than my compassion, and I sacrificed Miho to that fear.

Who can face that about themselves in eighth grade, when we are all made of fear? I couldn't. So even though I felt guilty when Miho went away, mostly I felt relieved to be free of the reminder of how I feared the way others might see me.

HINT

This guy comes up to me at a frat party. We talk. He's cute. He's attentive. He says, "Eriko. Is that Japanese?"

I say, "Yes."

He says, "I wondered if maybe you were Japanese."

I say, "Why?"

He says, "You have a hint of an accent."

I say, "No I don't. Unless it's a Minnesohhta accent." I hit the O hard, the way only a true Minnesotan can.

He says, "No, it's a Japanese accent."

BON-ODORI

It was the summer of camp and Starbucks. We went into town for Obon, the festival of the dead, when we welcome our ancestors home. I wore a yukata and wooden geta that my grandmother had bought just for me. As we walked, the geta rang out against the concrete, karin-korin, karin-korin. The sun had set, and the streets were lit with lanterns and lined with vendors hawking toys, grilled meat, and sweets. Hundreds of people danced in a slow, happy procession around a central dais to the sound of the tankō-bushi song blaring from the loudspeakers. Up on the platform, men playing taiko and shamisen accompanied the singer.

My grandmother taught me the words and helped me learn the steps:

Hotte, hotte, mata hotte!

Katsuide, katsuide atomodori!

It was a dance about mining for coal under the moon; dancers mimed digging, then swinging a sackful of coal over their shoulder, putting it in a cart, and letting it go. I moved my hands left, then right, clapped them together, swept them wide. I took four steps forward, then two steps back, two forward, then one back again.

We bought hanabi to take home with us, and crouched on

the street in front of the house and watched the tiny balls of orange fire spark and snap at the ends of the rice straws that we held in our hands. My grandmother served us glasses of barley tea and sent us inside to bathe and go to bed.

I could feel the tradition in my bones. When I close my eyes, can feel it still.

WHERE ARE YOU REALLY FROM?

I am from golden acres of wheat and cornfields, from towering mountain ranges and suburban subdivisions, from long, snaking rivers and ten thousand lakes. I am from political arguments with my dad at the diner. I am from long afternoons with my friends at the beach. This is my country. This is my birthright. This, despite what anyone says or thinks, despite my own doubts and fears and worries, is where I'm from.

I am from bright green squares of rice fields, from towns and cities chockablock with buildings, from glittering bays and busy harbors. I am from my grandfather's favorite soba shop, the one that's been there for a hundred years. I am from trips to the public bath with my mother. Japan is the land of my ancestors. This is where Miho was from. This is where my parents are from. This, despite what anyone says or thinks, despite all I've done to push myself away, is also where I'm from.

"Where are you really from?"

I know what people mean when they ask that question, and I can't—I won't—answer it the way they want, because "Japan" is not the truth. But "Minneapolis" is not the truth, either. All I can do is to ask back, "Where are you really from?"

ABOUT THE AUTHOR

~~~~~~~~~~~~~~~~~~~

MISA SUGIURA is the author of *It's Not Like It's a Secret*, winner of the 2018 APALA Literature Award for Young Adult Literature, and *This Time Will Be Different*, a 2019 Junior Library Guild selection and YALSA Best Books nominee. Her work has also appeared in the *New York Times*. Misa lives in California under a giant oak tree with her husband, two sons, two cats, and a gray-banded king snake named Pumpkin.

• • •

SALVATION AND THE SEA
Lilliam Rivera

• • •

I t was Leticia's idea. She got caught up watching the nineties movie *Thelma & Louise* on Netflix, over and over again. She especially replayed the part when Brad Pitt wasn't Brad Pitt but just a shirtless, fine, no-name cowboy who smashed Thelma. Leticia laughed whenever he spoke a line in the movie, giggling like she knew he wasn't that smart. Not me. I thought the movie was boring, dated, stuck in this strange space where the actresses tried to be all badass. It didn't feel real. Thelma and Louise shot up a guy, robbed a store, and put a cop in the trunk of his own patrol car, and all the while a detective tried his best to get them to surrender. They didn't get shot once. If you are white, even in a movie, you can get away with a lot.

Leticia didn't care. The minute the last scene of the two woman holding hands appeared on the screen, Leticia would start the film again.

"This film is so nineties," I said. "And so dumb."

"The nineties are back. Don't you know, stupid?" She grabbed my bottle of Coke and took a large sip from it.

Leticia wore a bandana around her neck. She rolled up her T-shirt to look more like Susan Sarandon, not that it worked. Leticia's thick, long black hair had absolutely no curl. She even thought of dying her hair red to go full-on Louise, but her mother would straight-up kill her, so she didn't. And wouldn't that make me Thelma, the ditzy best friend? I'm not ditzy. It's the other way around. Leticia is Thelma for sure, and I'm the one ready to kick a man in the balls.

Besides, Leticia's body was all curves like mine. Sometimes, when we stood side by side, randos would ask if we were related, as if all hermanas are family because we have the same hair color. As if we couldn't be more than just hermanas, maybe lovers or even frenemies, or whatever we wanted to be.

Randos and their labels.

"Is this it?" I asked.

Leticia kept staring at the movie, so I asked again.

"Is this it?"

It was Saturday, another Saturday, and I couldn't do this. I couldn't spend another day staring at this film that I could now recite lines from like the obsessive fan Leticia was becoming.

"We've got to do something," I said. "Go somewhere. Come on, Leti. Let's go to the swap meet."

There wasn't much to do at the swap meet. It wasn't as if we had much money between us. I had twenty dollars I'd stolen from my older brother's wallet when he wasn't looking. Leticia probably had less than that. But the luchadores practiced there on Saturdays, and our friend Pablo always snuck us in to watch. He'd been trying to get with me since we were in ninth grade and I let him make out with me in the back of his cousin's car. Pablo tried to play off like he didn't think about that night, but I could tell by the way his eyes twinkled when he saw me that he'd never forgotten having my tongue in his mouth.

I wasn't interested in Pablo or any of the luchadores. I just liked the attention. Leticia didn't mind it either, especially when they bought snacks or shared their edibles with us. At least the swap meet beat anything we were doing right now.

"I don't want to go to the swap meet," Leticia said. She adjusted her bandana and fished for her eyeliner to finish the bottom rim of her large eyes. "Let's do something different. Let's go somewhere new."

New? There's nothing new to do when you're broke. I prayed she didn't say go for a hike or some BS thing like seeing nature. Nature is not meant for girls like us. We're wild enough. I grabbed her eyeliner and practiced drawing a wingtip. The wing became longer and longer until I looked like an '80s punk rocker. Leticia rolled her eyes, not approving my look.

"Guess what?" she said, but I knew she wouldn't let me guess. I waited for her to spill it. "I got a gas card."

I smiled. With a gas card we could fill the tank of my crap car. A full tank meant freedom. Freedom to get the hell out of our dumb city and ignore the lustful luchadores and the disapproving abuelas and the infinite boredom. A full tank meant we had options. I didn't even want to ask how she'd gotten the card. Maybe from one of the luchadores last week, when we met them at the drive-in. Maybe it was her ama being kind, for once. It didn't matter. My car would soon have gas, and we could actually break out of this hell.

I pulled out my phone and popped up the Notes app to the list I'd been keeping of places to visit. Salvation Mountain was number one, right above Las Vegas and riding the Ferris wheel at Pacific Park in Santa Monica. Las Vegas was out of the question, because we needed more than twenty dollars to spend there. Santa Monica we could visit anytime, really, if we just planned it.

"Salvation Mountain," Leticia said with conviction. "We can take pictures and post them and make everyone jealous for not being us."

Leticia searched for images of Salvation Mountain. The trippy, neon-colored monuments were straight from a hippie's dream. So seventies and beautiful. I wanted to live there, to sleep besides the man-made folk art. I bet my dreams would become Technicolor too.

It was Leticia who'd found Salvation Mountain. She'd heard that the owner had recently died and that the art installation would soon die too. "Who's going to take care of it?" she'd asked, and I'd called her stupid for worrying about fake mountains so far away. Leticia swore her superpower was empathy. She claimed my superpower was being a total bitch and that was why we complemented each other.

She stared at the phone. Her fingerprints smudged the screen.

"We should go," she said.

"What if it's closed or something?" We could waste a perfectly good tank of gas for nothing. She typed on her phone and searched the 'gram. So many wannabes posing in front of the gigantic art installation. They wore their Coachella uniforms—cutoff jeans, fake flowers in their hair, ankle boots covered in dust. A fact was a fact: we didn't belong there. Not us dumb girls from El Monte with our ratty black T-shirts and our skinny jeans and our rolls of fat bulging out.

"I don't know," I said.

"Why not? You want to do something. This is what we can do," Leticia said. "We fill our water bottles and grab a couple snacks. We make sandwiches and head out right now. It will take about two and a half hours to get there."

The film was showing the part when Thelma and Louise are at a honky-tonk bar and people are line dancing. Cowboy boots pounded the floor in rhythm of the music. Leticia waited for me to respond.

"Okay, let's go," I said.

"Yesss, bish. We going fishin'!" Leticia screamed at the top of her lungs, doing a poor imitation of Thelma. Or was it Louise?

• • •

The first time I met Leticia, she offered me half of her tamale. We were both seven years old. It had been my first day of school, and I hadn't liked the school lunch so I'd refused to eat although my stomach growled loudly like a dog. Leticia didn't exactly offer the tamale, she thrust it at me, firmly telling me to eat like a mother would a child.

It didn't take long before Leticia and I were inseparable. We formed a barrier that no one could penetrate. Secrets told under bed sheets converted into tents. Shared meals and jokes. Of course, there was the one and only time we'd gotten pissed off at each other. We were twelve back then. Leticia had started to hang out with the girls who wore lipstick already, and I got angry. Those girls wanted to grow up way too fast. Eventually Leticia abandoned them and we were back on track, battling our days together.

Her parents worked in Vernon at the Farmer John factory, where they slaughter pigs. One time my parents and I drove past the factory, and it smelled like death. A truck had pulled up alongside of us and there they were, large pigs about to be driven to their annihilation. Their snouts poked out from the slits made for them to breathe. Leticia said the smell never left her parents' clothes. It was encrusted in their hands no matter how many bottles of perfume or cologne she gifted them for Christmas.

Every morning I tuned in to the news before heading to school to see how bad things were for Leticia and her parents. Green cards, citizenship interviews, documentations. Leticia was scared for her mom and dad, and I was nervous for Leticia. They'd left Guatemala so many years ago. They struggled to make a good life here in California like everybody else.

Still, when the man in the White House used the words *drug dealers, rapists,* and *animals,* Leticia didn't shrink. Her chest grew larger. We both stood tall and waited to see if anyone would repeat them words. One boy tried at school. He wasn't even white, just another brown boy like us. Angel. We cursed Angel out, both of us using the same words the man in the White House used. Others in the classroom joined in, and that felt good. We felt safe.

"If Angel thinks I'm an animal, I'll rip him apart like one," Leticia had said, and I'd believed her.

It was easy to scream at Angel when he used them hateful words. But the real fear came when we heard about families being ripped apart, even people we knew being rounded up and taken away. Curse words wouldn't protect Leticia and her family.

• • •

Although it was my car, Leticia claimed the radio. She was our DJ for the two hours until we reached Salvation Mountain. The bag of snacks stuffed in the tote bag rested by her feet for easy access.

"Let's listen to Ariana Grande," Leticia said.

We sang Ariana at the top of our lungs, the windows wide open, carrying our loud, out-of-tune singing voices to the cloudless blue sky.

"Why can't your car be a convertible?" Leticia asked. She tapped the Puerto Rican flag hanging off the dashboard. The flag was the symbol of my origin story: Puerto Ricans who ended up in California and so far away from the island. As for the car, it was a hand-me-down from my older brother, who'd practically run it into the ground.

"It nearly is. You don't see that?" I pointed to what looked like a bullet hole. My brother swore it was just a fluke, a rock that somehow penetrated the exterior of the car. I didn't believe him. "Don't complain. At least we have a car. I don't see you driving anything."

"When I have money I'm going to buy a convertible like the one Louise drives, and I'll get license plates that says Browngrlz 4ever."

"That's too many characters for a license plate, stupid," I said. Leticia snort-laughed, which made me laugh too.

The traffic slowed down a bit, and a man who looked like someone's tio in the car driving alongside of us stared, so I did what I did.

"What are you looking at?" I yelled.

"Mind your business, you ugly piece of…" Leticia added and we snort-laughed some more while the tio returned his attention to the road. We felt fearless. Bold. Like we could say and do whatever we wanted.

The first hour went fast. We could track the time from the albums we sang along to (Ariana and Bad Bunny) and the amount of snacks we ate. We talked about the dreams we had (I don't ever dream; Leticia's dreams are always about flying), and we talked about the best red lipstick ever made (Wet N Wild Cherry On Top). We didn't talk about the future, because that meant stress and I didn't want to invite stress into the car with us. More and more raids were occurring in Vernon, where her parents worked. Every day we wondered if the man in the White House would round up all the "maybe citizens" and lock them away. This was our constant fear. It forced us to create contingency plans. My parents' garage could shelter a family for a while, but a better idea would be to find a white family to hide them. We talked for hours, figuring out what we could do if the worst happened.

But not today. Today we were on an adventure.

"I see it!"

Leticia didn't hear me at first. She was too busy rapping along to Janelle, but I could see it. Salvation Mountain. It seemed to pop up out of nowhere on the long stretch of road.

"Wow," Leticia finally said. She even lowered the volume of the radio, as if the vibrant colors might sing out a melodious tune to welcome us and she didn't want to miss it. I slowed down to let the ethereal landscape come into focus, and then found a parking spot. We weren't the only ones who'd made the trek. The place was filled with people. Families and hipsters and tourists.

"You ready?" Leticia asked. She handed me Cherry On Top, and I adjusted the rearview mirror to reapply.

Whenever we arrived at a new space, Leticia and I had an unspoken rule. We entered with imaginary armor; armor that would protect us from questionable stares. We walked in at the ready, our lips pressed tightly together until the space was ours and we could smile widely.

Circles of girls wearing the typical music festival uniform posed in front of the waves of color. Leticia took hold of my hand, and we walked past them to the top of the mountain, right to the large sign in red that states God is Love. She stood in front of me, taking picture upon picture. Smiling. Serious. Silly face. Then it was her turn to make the same faces.

"Together," I said.

Leticia held the phone high so that it could include both of us and the extreme hues that enveloped us like colorful clouds. The sun kissed our skin. For those brief moments, we owned the celestial land.

"Let's explore," she said. We followed the yellow path down the monument and entered the cave-like rooms where so many objects were on display. My favorites were the old books and the sand-encrusted mirrors.

"If you had to live here, where would you sleep?" I asked.

Leticia wrinkled her nose and studied the room carefully. "Right here." She pointed to an elevated space made to look like a bench. "And you would sleep here." She pointed to the floor and laughed.

"You wish," I said, lightly pushing her.

Leticia found the perfect spot for us to eat our sandwiches, away from the crowd, underneath a tree painted in rainbow colors.

"I wish I had skills like an artist," she said. "I don't have any skills. I don't even know why I'm bothering going to school."

I shook my head. School would soon end, and with that came decisions that were made a few months ago: community college for Leticia, work for me. Leticia got this way, sometimes; she'd start to doubt herself, and that quickly became contagious, because I too would start to doubt myself.

"You're going to school because you're smart, stupid," I said. "Because your parents are busting their asses to make sure you do something other than work. Besides, you are not going that far. Take some classes, see what you like, and then keep moving forward. Pa'lante, remember?"

"Pa'lante. Right. You're not attending, and maybe that's why I'm nervous. Like, how am I supposed to follow when you are not right by me?" she asked. "What if I fail? What if I waste everyone's time and money?"

"What if you succeed? What about that? Stop saying no to yourself. If you win, I win. We are here to take over. Together."

She nodded. "You are right! We made it to Salvation Mountain." She paused. "It was a magical place on our list, and now we can scratch it off, because we got here. The magic is part of us. We can do anything."

I pointed at some posing white girls. "They don't know this yet, but we got this," I said. "All of it. We are going to win in spite of the walls and the dumb obstacles they place before us. We're warriors."

"Warrior hermanas," Leticia said. "We should get a tattoo right here." She pointed to her flexed arm, then pulled out her phone and added warrior hermana tattoos to our list.

"Here, eat." She handed me half of the Palomilla steak sandwich we'd picked up from Tito's Market. We finished our food and stayed another hour, until sunset. The drive back would have us hitting El Monte late. We had to go.

"The guy who made this, Leonard Knight, was such a religious freak," Leticia said as she read writings on the wall that declared peace and faith and temperance. "Everyone should live like this."

"Like religious people?" I asked. "Living righteously only works for people with money."

"No, you're wrong," she said. "We can live by these rules. Everyone can. If they took these words into their life, we wouldn't be in the situation we are now. People wouldn't be afraid of my family."

I didn't want to argue with Leticia. It was her tone. She needed to be right, so I let her be right. She took a picture of the sign, and we quietly walked back to the car.

• • •

To leave Salvation Mountain, we had to take the two-lane road towards Niland, California. When the cars in front of us slowed down, we knew there was trouble ahead of us. How was it that we hadn't noticed the roadblock on the way in? We'd been too busy singing, too busy rushing toward Salvation.

"They're checking," Leticia said. There was no panic in her voice, not yet. This wasn't the first time she'd had to deal with this. But we'd let our guard down, and now we were stuck behind these cars, inching closer to the men in uniform. "What if they take me in? What's our plan?"

"Don't say a word. I will talk." We hadn't done anything wrong, and we had to maintain that feeling because fear would get us nowhere. "We're good."

The closer we got to the checkpoint, the tighter my hands gripped the steering wheel. We were not even close to the border, but here they were, ICE, doing what they did best. Leticia pulled down the mirror and placed her hair up in a bun. Her lipstick still glistened red. The car in front of us was full of a bunch of girls we'd seen earlier, taking pictures in front of the mountains, just like us, except they were white.

One of the patrolmen talked while the others looked on menacingly. Jokes must have been exchanged, because one of the girls flicked her hair back and laughed. Leticia connected her phone to the car charger. She practiced her smile, as did I. I stopped the car in front of the line of border patrol cops. One of them held a leash connected to a large German shepherd.

"Who here is Puerto Rican?" he asked, pointing to the miniature flag hanging off the dashboard.

"We both are," I said. Big smiles. I turned to Leticia and she nodded.

"Too bad," another patrolman teased. I focused on the one in front me, but sometimes glanced over—to the dog, to the men wearing sunglasses that shielded their eyes. Their mirrored sunglasses reflected my face.

"My family is from Bayamon, but we moved to Los Angeles. Silly, right? We should have stayed near the beach." I spoke too fast. His name tag said Ortiz.

"Where are you from?" I asked. Beside me Leticia shifted. Her leg bounced nervously.

"Mexico," he said. A patrolman led the dog around my car. My gaze went to Ortiz's badge and the revolver that clung to his hip.

"You're an Ortiz. That's my mother's name," I said, clearly becoming more and more like ditzy Thelma. "We could be related."

"No," he said with finality, and he was right, because he had the gun and all I had were my stupid words. We smiled at each other. "So, you're not even really Puerto Rican. You were born here."

And I joked, "So?" But he shook his head, because I'd failed his test. The cop who stood behind him didn't grin at all. His hand rested on his belt buckle. I continued to talk. Tell jokes. Flirt.

"And you?" he asked Leticia. She looked straight at me, her smile intact.

"I'm from Bayamon too," she said. "We're cousins."

He stared at her for a long moment. My hands still clutched the wheel. My knuckles turned white.

"Where are you going?"

"Back to El Monte," she said. "We're going home."

The patrolman with the dog finished his inspection. He stood alongside the others. No smile. No recognition at all. The man with the Ortiz name tag did the head nod, alerting us we were free to go. I shifted the car from Park into Drive. Leticia didn't turn the radio back on. We continued in silence. I watched the roadblock recede behind us.

My heart was pounding so hard that my whole body seemed to shake with each beat. So many things raced through my head, words I should have said or not said. Had I smiled too much? I must have looked like a fool, like a parrot spouting nonsense. I couldn't even look at Leticia, because I could feel it. I could sense her fear, and it was bound to explode.

"Puerto Rico. Do I look Puerto Rican to you?" she asked. Venom underscored her tone, and I understood why.

"What? Would it have been better for him to figure out you're Guatemalan?" I asked. "I didn't know what I was saying. I just wanted him to let us go."

"His stupid face. His stupid grin. The way he talked like all he had to do was ask for ID." Her voice trembled a little, because she was angry, like me. So angry that I wanted to cry.

"He didn't though. He let us go, so we beat them. We tricked them."

Leticia shook her head. "It's so easy for you. You can come and go. You never have to worry," she said. Her words stung.

"It's not my fault I'm Puerto Rican," I said. Puerto Rican means nothing, just ask the reality show host living in the White House. Just ask my family back on the island, who worry about their jobs and keeping their houses. But Leticia was right. I could move around. We'd left the island and found something better. Leticia's family had left Guatemala with the same hope, and yet a simple checkpoint could mean the end for her.

"I was just trying to get us out of there," I said. "Did you see the way they were looking at us? How the dog was looking at us, like it knew?" I said this loudly, because she needed to believe me. I hadn't noticed how my foot was pressing down on the gas pedal. I was speeding. I thought about that time she'd told me about her cousins having to duck down in the car to avoid getting pulled over. How they wouldn't travel to San Diego or anywhere near the border.

"I'm tired of hiding, of my parents having to pretend everything is fine while people around them think California is safe," Leticia said. "I'm tired of having to look down at the floor when a cop talks to me."

"But I have to look at the floor too," I said, needing to defend myself. "We're warrior sisters, aren't we? We are in this battle together."

"You don't know what it's like," she said. "It's easy for you. My dreams aren't of flying. They are nightmares of being locked away in a windowless cell."

I rubbed away tears, but they kept flowing.

"I hate this life," she said. "We can't just get in a car and be free like Thelma and Louise. A stupid movie about white women." She took off her bandana and tossed it out the window.

I didn't know what to say. I felt ashamed for flirting with the border patrolmen, for doing what I had to do. Things are easy for me and my family. I'd be dumb to think otherwise, to believe that, because we are both brown, the world isn't playing favorites when it clearly does.

I spotted the sign that read Salton Sea. I needed to get out of the car—it felt too crowded with emotions. I parked and didn't bother letting Leticia know what I was doing, just opened the door and got out. Leticia soon followed. Flies circled us. The ground crunched as if we were walking on bones. Tiny bones. There was no one around to witness our sneakers crushing the stones to dust. Leticia was angry, and I didn't know how to reach her or how to make things better. Leticia's superpower was empathy, but my superpower sucked.

"It smells like death," she said after a long silence.

"Yeah," I said.

I didn't grab Leticia's hand. I just stood by her. We stared at the desolate Salton Sea and waited for a sign to point us back home.

ABOUT THE AUTHOR

LILLIAM RIVERA is an award-winning writer and author of the young adult novels *Dealing in Dreams*, *The Education of Margot Sanchez*, and *Never Look Back*. Her work has appeared in the *Washington Post*, the *New York Times*, and *Elle*, to name a few. Lilliam lives in Los Angeles.

• • •

VOLVIÉNDOME

Alaya Dawn Johnson

• • •

It's different, every time I go back. The very familiarity makes it strange to me, as though I have fallen asleep to travel the old corridors of my half-forgotten childhood, where my friends and family and I slide into our grooves, side-by-side troughs in the sediment of the last thirty years, so deep that we can hardly see one another. But I am not asleep as I land in National (we old Washingtonians who remember our loyalties still refuse to use that bastard's name). I am awake and my skin feels inside out, rasping like a hair shirt, as I step onto the gate bridge. The air is thick and sweet, the sun weak; I am stepping across a chasm, into another time, another life. I was born in DC, and I spent my twenties in New York, but five years ago I packed two suitcases and fled across the border. I remade myself: I learned Spanish, found kindred spirits among my fellow displaced, diasporic artists of

Mexico City, entered a master's program to sit with ancient texts in old languages and dream of the past. I liked so much of the person I was becoming that I began to flinch from the girl I had been. Her places were not my own.

And yet, I have landed. I try not to think about what I have come here to do. It's an old trick: some decisions, however necessary, must be left to the edges of your thoughts until you have already jumped; then, they can be grieved.

I think of Mexico instead—evening downpours, the morning trash bell, atole and tamales for breakfast, the old sun, the burning eye. But everyone else wants to get off the plane; my past pushes me forward. It's different every time I go back, but this feeling of being two in one, a snake required at regular intervals to slide back into a dry and raspy skin—this is the same.

It is—a kind of—home.

● ● ●

I was nineteen years old, about to go on my third date with an older man. He had convinced me to give him my email address at a political rally that I was covering for my university newspaper. He had said, "Do you want to have your most interesting interview of the night?" I was feeling both overwhelmed and beautiful. He was too old for me, thirty-six, but I told myself I didn't care. At least he was interesting. He had a kind of totalizing presence that comforted me with its familiarity, even though I halfheartedly bit back. The grooves were already there; his genius had just been to find them and make himself at home. We went to the restaurants that he wanted, listened to the seventies bands that he liked, and he lectured me on the big-name leaders of the US political left that had been neglected in my Washington DC private school education: Noam Chomsky, Alexander Cockburn, Eric Foner, Howard Zinn. A bunch of white men, but when I called him on it, he said, reprovingly, that no white man was more anti-racist than he was. Didn't he love black women?

That afternoon, before the older man picked me up from in front of my dorm, my mother called me.

"I just wanted you to know that your father has decided to leave E——."

"What do you mean, leave? As in, he no longer believes in our religion?"

"He's had a series of revelations. And he's decided that while it has many good elements, it isn't the true path."

"So, he just, what, raised us to believe in this not-true path for the last nineteen years, and now he's like, whoops, my mistake? Was he planning to tell me this?"

"I'm sure your father wants to talk to you about his next steps. He is using his spiritual tools to create a new path."

"He's starting his own religion?"

"It isn't a religion. It's a spiritual path to higher conscious-ness."

I must have said something. I must have said goodbye. The words of my childhood had softened and then rotted in my mouth. I had been struggling with my faith for the last year; I had left the holy book on my shelf where it seemed to glow with the toxic shame of my inadequacy, of my obstinate need to judge its contents and find them not just unbelievable, but offensive. Dad had told me that I was just too spiritually under-developed, that the brilliance of the text would make itself clear to me as I surrendered myself to God and our spiritual leader.

The god and spiritual leader that he had apparently decided were a big lie about two weeks ago. Only now had my mother bothered to tell me. Dad had been the highest-ranking Spiritual Aide in the region when we were growing up. He would wake us up at five in the morning every weekday for prayer services before school. He would criticize our spiritual development, our inability to fully practice the doctrine.

I told the older man on our date. I made it a joke. "Can you believe that my mom called just to casually inform me that my dad left his cult—the one he raised us in—to found his own? So, I guess I've lost my religion?"

He told me that he was agnostic. I liked the sound of that. I didn't want to hear another word about my spiritual goddamn development for the rest of my life, I decided it that very night. We went to some East Village concert, in some bar where they ought to have ID'd me but the older man convinced the bouncer I had left mine behind. He was charming, practiced, persuasive in his conviction to get whatever he wanted. It was a familiar dynamic, but more pleasant: what he wanted was to show me his world. As long as it was nothing like my own, I would take it, hold it until my hands bled and I forgot why I clung so tightly in the first place. I knew only that I had to hold on, or I would have to face myself, a kind of death.

● ● ●

I went to Mexico for the first time a few months before I finally broke things off with the older man. After eight years, the pressure of his presence, once so comforting in its familiarity, weighted down my very organs. I felt as though I were facedown on a glue trap. If I stayed I knew where I would end: the self-hypnotizing handmaiden to a demagogue. Ag-

nostic white savior or latter-day black messiah did not make
as much of a difference to the fundamental dynamic as I had
imagined at nineteen. I went to Mexico with my sister, and
I began to breathe again. We spent our days climbing ruins.
We climbed the baths of Nezahualcoyotl, the poet-king of
Texcoco, who would take to the waters in the rocky hills
above his mist-shrouded city and contemplate the death of
all of his glory: Annochipa tlalpac. Zan achica ye nican / Tel
ca chalchihuitl no xamani no teocuitlatl in tlapani no quet-
zalli potztequi / Annochipa tlalpac. Zan achica ye nican. (Not
forever on this earth, only here for a little while/ Even jade
shatters, even gold cracks, even quetzal plumes fall to pieces/
Not forever on this earth, only here for a little while)

A little stone frog squatted on the edge of one bathing pool,
a worn-down stump where his face used to be. We climbed
over the terraced hillside, the earth fragile and crumbly with
the ash of a recent slash-and-burn. I imagined these baths
the way they would have looked to Nezahualcoyotl, volcanic
stone whitewashed and decorated green and blue, running
with clear waters that would have reflected the thousand colors of the day and night. I imagined the farmland surrounding them, the terraced maize fields much like the ones we
hiked through in our tourist's sandals. The maize would push
up from the lunar black and gray, green stalks covered with a
fine down, diamond-studded in the morning fog and green
as jade when the sun blinks its eye. The rains would end, and
ears golden, sapphire and onyx would be struck from stalks,
hung in garlands in storerooms and local temples. And those
selfsame stalks, old and brown now, would fall to the earth
in a great burning, to be reborn, like Quetzalcoatl, with the

morning star. I did not know any of that then. I was busy dying, as it turned out, in preparation.

We would drag our dusty feet back into the city that night, eat the cheapest food we could find in La Condesa (not very cheap) and collapse in our hostel bed. Every night I was assailed by terrors. I could barely feel my body. I could barely think. I dreamed of rat mazes, endless turns and dead ends and no possible escape until I awoke, heart pounding. And yet I was cradled in the unknown speech of this place, the languages that I did not know and whose very mystery cleared my throat of words I no longer believed. Among the old bones of civilizations lost to the earth, that old skin of an ancient crocodile, the hard knot in the wet rag of what had been my heart eased just a little. I thought to myself—a voice from the other end of the wormhole, my own self screaming back in time, a signal flare—I could live here.

• • •

I was seventeen the first time I left home for a place unfamiliar to me. It rolled me over and raised my head. I did not know then what was air and what was earth, only that I longed to breathe.

My father and I traveled to Nigeria to dedicate a new temple in a coastal city. My father had been instrumental in bringing the teachings of our religion to West Africa, and when we arrived, I realized that while he had been an important person in the small cult world of Washington, DC, in Nigeria he was someone much bigger. They had photos of him everywhere. They wanted his blessing, his words. As his daughter, the holy aura extended to me, an uncomfortable, sticky glow. Dad wanted me to reflect well upon him. I was required to sing religious songs (mostly American classics tackily redone with spiritual lyrics) twice a day during the services. I met some other teens. One, Tope, was particularly fun to be around. I escaped my minder—an earnestly religious woman in her forties whom I perceived as trying far too hard to be jolly and good-natured, and who was, I am now sure, merely trying to do her job corralling a confused and rebellious American girl. I told her that I needed to use the bathroom and escaped through the window while she waited patiently outside the door. Tope and I bought ice pops from a local vendor and walked around the giant compound. The main temple was mostly finished, but the parishioners had planned a monumental complex to honor the spiritual teachings that my father had helped bring to this country. We walked among the concrete block foundations of various outbuildings, much as I would walk among the ruins of ancient temples years later in Mexico: imagining what they would be, imagining what they had been. Bones exist not of themselves but as representations of potential, past or future. They are a being reduced to its bleached essence. But it is flesh, so briefly animated, that makes those bones dance, resplendent in gold and jade. It is hope, and then death.

Tope told me that he had always dreamed of a girl like me; the girls here, he said, weren't spiritual enough for him. I must chant my prayers every day; I must speak directly with our spiritual master.

I didn't have the words to tell him the truth. I was running from my father in those ruins. I was looking at those cinderblock bones and imagining the flesh of a different kind of life. Two years later, when I met the older man, he played me some songs by Richie Havens. I became obsessed; I listened to his best-of album hundreds of times. And I wrote, from inside that older man's world, which would never be my own, Richie Havens, late at night/ Is searching for his dolphins/ while I'm searching for my father.

• • •

There are only five hours between my old life and the new; five hours, or eighteen years. It's time to jump.

I have come back to visit the older man one last time. My birthday is tomorrow; I am now older than he was when he first met me, a month after 9/11. I cannot imagine dating a nineteen-year-old; my whole being balks at the idea. He has been keeping the last of my things in the US in his basement. But he has a new girlfriend now, and she doesn't like seeing these relics of me in his house. I could tell her: the house is nothing but relics, old sediment that accretes and hides the cockroaches. The books in the bathroom—entirely tiled in black—are the same ones that were there a decade ago, when I first left.

This is the last time I will leave. I have brought two friends with me. Old friends, who understand more than I have said about these sticky men in my life, my lifelong flight. Home, an automatic mantra of these days when I am overwhelmed and at sea. Home—both curse and current of deepest longing. We throw out a lifetime of dust in an hour and a half: boxes of books, written by others and written by me, old copyedited manuscripts, my first unpublished novel that I spent an entire summer editing on the older man's couch. I learned how to write that summer. I was all alone in a sticky trap, but I was becoming, even then. The woman who got out, who found a place where she could breathe and so learned to speak—she was living inside of that girl, waiting.

I see that girl as we paw through her things, careless in

our haste. The older man places himself between me and my friends, as though it is his animal nature, even now, to isolate me from any other support. "Don't you want to keep this?" he asks, "Are you sure you want to throw this away? You can leave this here, Snoozly."

I hate when he calls me that. I have always hated it. I took it like medicine.

I look at the stuff of this girl, most I will throw away, and some I will keep. I love her, in that moment, in a way that she could never love herself. I love her for trying. I can even understand her staying. You don't live here anymore, I tell her, when it's over, when I am in my friend's car with the last of the boxes, shaking and crying, I'm taking us home.

●●●

Thursday morning, the sun has just poked its shoulders over the mountains. The burning eye is lidded, sleepy. My thesis defense is today. I'm awake. The air is dry, the cars are quiet. Beside me, my partner shifts and rests his hands in the valley between my rib cage and my hip. The garbage truck comes early; the bell peals below our window, close now and then more distant, as the man walks up and down the street. The garbage bell is the first note of the symphony of the day. Soon will come the flute of the knife sharpener, a lonely trill, a descending scale that ends on a minor note, the ghost call of Tenochtitlan's migratory birds. Then the junk collector truck, with its iconic cry: se compra, colchones, tambores, refrigeradoras, estufas… The gas men with their deep bellows and the drum of tanks rolled over the sidewalk. The brassy tinkle of the sweet wafers and the clown-car toot of bread and pastries.

Five hundred years ago, the lake of the Basin of Mexico was

a vibrant expanse, crisscrossed by aqueducts and highways and plots of land built-up over the lake bed. Canoes navigated the canals, through houses and temples and intensive farm-plots and open markets, where you could still buy tamales and atole in the morning, or pulque, or candied squash dripping with honey; bells would ring through the streets and conch shells would sing the hour and the sun, that burning eye, would stare lidless down at the world of their creation. Even then, there would have been people like me. People who escaped to Tenochtitlan, the most beautiful city in the world, to live again.

I head to the university with my friends. A few minutes before we all go into the exam room, I walk to the balcony and look out over the south of the city. The smog has lifted this morning, and the mountains are clear. I feel, as I do every time I see them, a gut punch of relief, a longing and a peace, the knowledge that I am now very far from where I was. My best friend from high school is here with me, and my partner. She who knows me where I came from and he who knows me where I am. I cannot give up that other place, but I have been learning to release my grip. I bring the girl with me when I stand in front of my committee and present the work that has been my passion for the past three years. She knows how to stand, knows how to speak in public. Her father gave her that. There is so much love in the world. We had to go far away, learn to breathe in a different language, just to articulate it. The exam concludes. My friends and I all go into the hallway again to await the results. I sit on the floor with my head between my knees, swaying with the weight I have carried for so long and now released. I have my flesh, my bones, the dizzying view from all the years I have climbed like mountains.

ABOUT THE AUTHOR

ALAYA DAWN JOHNSON has published seven novels for adults and young adults, including *The Summer Prince*, longlisted for the National Book Award, and *Love Is the Drug*, winner of the Nebula award. Her latest is the historical adult novel, *Trouble the Saints*. She was born in Washington, DC, and spent thirteen years in New York before migrating to Mexico City, where she now makes her home. She received her master's degree in Mesoamerican Studies from the Universidad Nacional Autónoma de México in April of 2019, with honors.

● ● ●

THE TRIP
Sona Charaipotra

● ● ●

Today's the day. I can feel it in my bones. Well, okay, not my bones. But my dil. The way my heart has been racing all morning, speeding up even more every time I'm within five feet of Rajan—and I will be, for the next ten days. I know something big is about to happen. And I can't wait.

"Everyone got their passports ready?" Professor Hollander asks as she starts handing out boarding passes. Ten days, twelve teens, and two (decidedly lax) chaperones. I feel like I need to pinch myself, like they do in the movies. Or like there are bees in my stomach instead of butterflies. This incessant buzzing of heat and energy. Like I'm on the edge of something, and totally ready to fall off.

I still can't believe it's finally here. I've been looking forward to this trip for two years, since I first moved to Westwood High as a freshman and joined the model UN team.

Geneva. For a whole week. I've never been anywhere. Except for India, of course.

But this is different. For once, I get to be just the average girl. No parental supervision. No chores or drama from Nanima, who likes to stalk my every move, like she's my mother, not Mom's. I still don't quite know how Mom convinced her to let me go, although I overheard several murmured discussions over late-night cups of chai. And then Mom said it was okay. I barely survived the month before the trip, I was so bursting with excitement.

Now it's here: a week exploring and having fun, completely parent (and Nani!) free. And well, the whole presentation thing, too. With my best friends. And Rajan. Though I'm probably more excited about that part than he is. We've been practicing our talk for a month, and I think he's finally starting to realize I'm a girl. Maybe.

He'll definitely know after this trip. I packed and repacked my bag all weekend, plotting out each outfit, so he'll have no choice but to think of me as more than just his debate project partner. And this morning, a little kajal, a shiny lip gloss, and, for good measure, those pale blue glass bangles he kept commenting on last week.

"Hey Sarika," Rajan says, coming up behind me on the security line, touching one of the bangles. He's staring down at me from behind those unruly curls that keep landing in his line of vision, that too-wide grin making me blush before I can even say a word. "What seat are you?"

I look down at the ticket Hollander handed me. "23C." I smile, trying my best not to actually beam.

"Oh, I'm 23E. Maybe I'll make Mike switch." He grins.

"Then we can go over our segment. I mean, it is an eight-hour flight."

"I'm gonna sleep," Mike says with a groan. "So you guys better keep it down."

Rajan raises a brow and smirks. "I make no promises," he says, and Mike punches him lightly in the shoulder.

"Come on," Hollander shouts in our direction, and we all scoot to catch up with the group. The security line winds for miles behind us, even though it's barely 6:00 a.m. The thought of getting lost in this crowd sends a shiver through me. I've never traveled solo before. I mean, I'm on a school trip, so it's not really solo. But no parents. It's surreal, the freedom of it. Even if Hollander is kind of hovering.

"Andy will take half the group, and you five stick with me," Hollander says, waving to me and a few others. I watch Rajan and his friends shuffle off behind Andy. But Neha and Beck stay put, so I guess I should, too. I pull my laptop out of my bag, along with my stash of snacks, and dump them into the security bins.

I throw my backpack onto the conveyor belt and walk toward the little security gate.

Andy and his group—including Rajan—are through in about ten minutes, but we're in a different and apparently much slower line. Hollander hands our passports over to the guy at the desk, who scans each one, frowning the whole time. He hands her back a bunch but keeps one. Hollander pushes us forward.

The woman behind the counter scans every bag from top to bottom, rummaging through each one even when the scanner brings up nothing, and rerouting about half of them for further checking. Sigh. One by one, we go through the full body scanner, lifting our arms and shedding our dignity.

My underwire triggers the thing, as usual, and the uniformed, blonde woman behind the gate waves me over for a pat-down. Funny how no one else's bra ever causes such drama.

"Remove your necklace, please," Faux-Ever Blonde says, and I slip off my little Ganesh chain and place it in the round bin the lady holds out. He's the god of new beginnings and so very necessary for this trip. Plus, Nani gave him to me, so I feel a little pinch as the lady shoves the bin onto the conveyor and I watch Ganeshji disappear.

The woman runs her small electronic scanner over me, from head to toe, and waves it twice over the offending underwire. She's blonde, though her brows are decidedly brunette, and she doesn't crack a single smile, even though I greet her with my best. I grin, trying to put us both at ease. But apparently that was the wrong move. Faux-Ever Blonde runs it down my leg again, and we discover the real culprit. My payal, sitting sweet and elegant against my ankles. What was I thinking? But I know exactly what I was thinking. Rajan thinks they're sexy. At least, that's what Beck claims.

"I'll take them off," I say with a sigh, leaning down and removing the offending anklets one by one.

The lady's still frowning. "Name?" she asks, and I raise a brow. Oh god, not today.

"Sarika Shah."

"Where are you headed, miss?"

"Geneva." Sweat pools at my neck and slides down my back. I want to wipe at it, but I can't risk any sudden moves. I try to smile. Why am I worried? "School trip."

She scans over my bra again, then uses her palm to do another pat-down. I frown.

"I'm going to ask you to stand to the side for a moment," she says. I step out of the cube and spot Beck and Neha, waiting just outside the security gate. Thank god they didn't leave me behind.

But they've got their bags already, and Neha looks pointedly at her watch. I shuffle from one foot to the other and peer at the conveyor belt, hoping they've already grabbed my stuff. Well, my laptop at least. It's not there.

The rest of the group is gathered and ready to go. I point to the conveyer, and Beck shrugs. I don't think my bag has come out yet. I stand there, trying to keep the panic from hitting my face.

"Boarding starts in half an hour," Ms. Hollander announces to the group. "So if you need a bathroom break or coffee, it's now or never. Meet me in front of Gate 32 in twenty."

"We'll wait for Sari," Neha says, and Hollander nods before heading toward the ladies' room.

Where's my laptop? It has all my notes on it. I start to move forward to check, but the security lady comes out then, frowning. "Just a minute, miss."

She's got my bags. Behind the counter. Dammit.

"You ready?" Beck says, pulling her backpack onto her shoulder. "I want a frappuccino before we board."

I look at the lady behind the counter, who's still rifling through my bag. I shrug. "Go. I'll meet you at the gate."

I stand around, watching Faux-Ever Blonde dig through my stuff, and frown as the boarding time edges closer and closer. She studiously avoids my gaze, then looks up and scowls at me. "Can I see your passport, miss?" she demands, hand out and mouth stern. I reach for my money pouch, where I keep my passport, and realize I don't have it. Hollander does. Or maybe it was the one they kept?

"I—um, I don't know—it's not with me." I stutter as I say the words.

She glares my way a second, then storms back toward the security booth.

Faux-Ever Blonde talks to the man who scanned our passports earlier—he's still frowning, too. He shuffles through a batch he has on his desk and pulls one out. Is that my passport? Weird. That can't be a good sign.

It's inevitable now. I'm going to miss the boarding window. And no one has come back to find me. The woman seems to be long gone, my passport MIA with her. And my phone, I realize with a start. It's with the rest of the stuff in the scanner. So I can't even call to let Hollander know I'm still here.

Everyone around me is moving on along, not noticing my silent panic. I have no phone, no ID, and no chaperone to come and resolve this.

Do not freak, I keep telling myself. Beck and Neha will be back as soon as they realize I'm still MIA. Right? Maybe another minute, or five, tops.

But where did that woman go with my passport and boarding pass? There's someone else scanning bags now, and another uniformed lady is doing the pat-downs. What if that lady wasn't a TSA employee at all, but a random passport thief who somehow managed to get into the security booth? No. That's super unlikely. It's probably just a case of classic racial profiling. I mean, it's not like I haven't been stopped before.

But usually I'm with my mom and family, and not just by myself. Especially these days, with all this bullshit with the Muslim ban and stuff. It's definitely that. They think I'm a terrorist. Because I so look like a terrorist at all of five feet tall, with my hair in old-school braids, and short-alls to go with my vintage 'NSync T-shirt.

I'm staring at my feet, fretting about what to do, when a shadow falls over me. Oh, Hollander, thank god.

Except it's not Hollander at all. "Miss, we need you to come with us."

It's a short, stocky white dude in a suit. He's got close-cropped brown hair, and his face is grim. I mean, his whole demeanor is grim. Like he's a reaper from one of those TV shows. Except not sexy.

Hollander shows up just as I'm walking away. "Where are you taking her?" she shouts after us, but as far as I know, nobody bothers to respond. I wave, frantic, hoping she takes that as a signal that I'll be right out. I'm probably holding up the flight.

I follow the cranky man and blonde lady to a bank of cubicles just outside the security gate area. They're all unmarked and gray, like prison cells in some dystopian novel. I know there's something I should do or say right now. Refuse to speak unless accompanied by a lawyer, right? Or at least an actual adult. But the woman just nudges me along, her mouth a straight line of nothingness, all business, as we follow Meanie.

The man opens the door to one of the nondescript cubes, and I falter, but the lady pushes me in. "Sit."

I take a seat at a wooden table as the guy sits across from

me, the woman hovering by the door. A single bulb lights the cube, but just barely. I glance around the room, and spy my stuff stashed in one corner, the suitcase flung open, the contents of my backpack shoved into a bin. I open my mouth to speak, then shut it. On Mom's favorite cop drama, the perp never speaks first. I suppress a nervous giggle. Or maybe it was a hiccup. When did I become the perp?

I stare down at the dark, scratched wood of the table. I wipe my clammy palms on my cargo pants, but there's nothing I can do about the drop of sweat that's sliding down my cheek like a tear.

If Meanie thinks I'm crying, he clearly doesn't care.

"What's your name?" he asks, in a super gruff tone that makes me sit up at attention, like I did at my citizenship interview four years ago.

I flinch but hold my voice steady. "Sarika Shah."

"Age?"

"Sixteen."

"Social?"

Like Twitter? Or Insta?

The man glares. "Do you have a social security number?" he asks again, slowly, like I don't understand English.

Oh. "Yeah. Of course. It's 999-732-1380." I swallow hard. "Can you, like, call my teacher. Ms. Hollander? I'm gonna miss my flight."

"Where are you from?" Meanie asks, ignoring my questions.

"Westwood. New Jersey. Twenty-five minutes from here."

"No, where are you really from?"

"I live at 11 Maiden Lane, Westwood, NJ." I sigh. "I think I should call my parents."

"And you've lived there…"

"Two years. No, three. Like two and a half?" I look toward Faux-Ever Blonde, who's leaning in the doorway, busy scrolling on her phone. I wonder what time it is.

"Where did you live before that?" Meanie asks.

"Jersey City. We got priced out. And my mom got married."

"And your mom is?"

"Ambika Shah. I mean, Ambika Sharma, now. My Nanima is Gulmohar Shah. My stepdad, they got married three years ago. Nitesh Sharma. From Jersey City. By way of Jalandhar."

"Your English is very good."

"Thanks. I get As in it, mostly. And I'm on the debate team."

"Where's your accent?"

"I'd say my only accent is Jersey."

"But you were not born here?"

"No. We moved when I was two."

"Not Indian."

"Well, yes. And no." Shit. I'm sweating now, because this is serious. They really do think I'm a terrorist. Based on one word on my passport. One word. The circumstance of my birth. My family is from Kashmir. Disputed territory. With a large Muslim population. But I haven't been there since I was a baby, when my mom and Nanoo escaped here, seeking asylum.

"Have you been to your country recently?"

"I'm a US citizen."

"Have you been to your country recently?"

I swallow hard. "Define recently."

The man sighs. "Let me put it another way—what interaction have you had recently with people from your country?"

Again, my country? "I'm an American." I gesture toward my passport, which sits on the table between us, just out of my reach. "You know that."

"Listen, Ms. Shah, I don't want any trouble. But your family history and place of birth when we did the scan flagged you in our system. We've been ordered to hold you—and your passport—for further vetting."

"But I'll miss my flight."

"So you'll miss your flight."

I place my hands on the table, trying not to fidget, working not to cry. "Can I call my parents?" I mean, even criminals get one phone call. Right?

"No. Sit tight. We'll be back shortly." He stands abruptly and walks out, taking the blonde with him.

I sit in the dimly lit cubicle for a minute, then two, then ten. No one returns. I wonder if they even remember I'm in here. I wonder where Hollander is. I wonder if my parents know. I've probably missed the flight. Would they just leave without me?

I scan the cubicle. There's no clock. Nothing to give me any idea how long I've been in here as time ticks by. But my bag is in the corner. And my laptop is in the bin. I wonder if my phone is in there too. I stare at the door, willing it to open. Then I stare at it some more, wondering if I should risk it. I have to. If I can call Mom, she'll know what to do.

I tap the table and then grab my leg, trying to get it to stop shaking. I need to do something. I can't just sit here and wait for them to come back and interrogate me some more. Who knows what other nonsense they'll come up with? These days, they'll use any excuse to deport people. Especially brown people. Even citizens.

If I get caught going through my things, that might just give them the excuse they need. But it seems like they're going to do what they want, whether it's legal or not. So I might as well do what I need to do, too.

I stand, looking frantically around the room. What if there's a camera, I realize too late. But now that I'm up, I have to move.

I'm definitely going to miss the flight. I'm going to miss Geneva, and hanging out with my friends, and making my speech, and maybe making out with Rajan. I'm going to miss prom and graduation and college and living my American dream. Everything I've worked so hard for. Everything that I've been dreaming about for days and months and years. All the reasons my family fought so hard to be here. All because of where I was born. A place I never really knew, a place I'll probably never see again. My heart is racing and my eyes are wet, tears ready to spill, but I won't cry. Nope. I have to stay calm.

Slowly, quietly, I tiptoe toward the corner of the room, where my stuff is scattered. As soon as I'm there, I turn back toward the door. No one. Thank god. I start to comb through the bin, looking for my phone. Or at least my ID. Definitely my passport. None of them are in my suitcase, which holds only the dresses and outfits I'd picked out oh, so carefully, hoping to impress Rajan. The thought makes me laugh now, though it's a high-pitched, hysterical yelp of a thing. I can't believe I let myself get excited. It was too good to be true. The bees that were buzzing so sweetly before are full-on stingers now, and my stomach roils like it's being attacked by a swarm.

I have to find something, anything that will help me prove who I am when they finally accuse me of being a terrorist. Because they definitely will. I've seen this happen too many times, on TV, on the news, and I've even heard stories from people at the temple. It doesn't matter that I'm sixteen, that I grew up here in New Jersey, that I haven't touched Indian soil in years. It doesn't matter that I'm a straight A student, that I'm on the Presidential Honor Roll, that my future will be as lawyer or a TV correspondent.

Well, I'll definitely be news now.

This is it. That story you always see. Came here when I was two. A total Jersey girl. All-American.

Except that I was born in a region marked for "further vetting" or "possible terrorist ties." In a nation I've barely known and may never get to see again. Unless they deport me tomorrow.

That's when the shaking starts. Slow at first, a slight tremor in my hands. But soon I can't control it. Then the tears come in a flood, the sobs wracking me from head to toe. And I can't make it stop, no matter what. My mind is spiraling out of control, the stories that Nani told me about bombs on Dal Lake and the army taking over schools and homes scrambling any rational thought. I try deep breaths, and counting, and staring at a random spot on the wall. But I can't stop thinking about how I'll never see my mom or Nani again, about how maybe they won't even know where to look for me. I have to pull myself together. I can't let Meanie and the

blonde find me here, lying on the cold linoleum in a dim
room, sobbing.

I sit up and try the deep breaths again. I will myself to stand
and cross the room, one step at a time, making my way back
to the table. I'm nearly there when the door opens, creaking
ominously, the dim light casting Meanie's shadow across the
floor. I shudder, and I hear him laugh.

"Just a misunderstanding, of course," he says with another
boom of laughter. And then I see the other shadow, small and
slim, cast alongside his. Hollander. Thank god.

She pushes past the man and reaches me first, and I sort of
collapse into her, even though I've never so much as high-
fived her before.

"Are you okay?" she shouts, practically shaking me. "I was
so worried. They wouldn't tell me where you were, or why
they took you. They wouldn't let me talk to Agent Lombardi
here until I threatened to call the governor's office. Lombardi
is from ICE. But your passport clearly states you are a US citizen." She's stroking my back now, as my tears soak her T-shirt.
I've never been more happy to see another human in my life.
"Your mom was frantic." That just makes me sob harder. My
mom. I need to talk to my mom. "Thank god you're okay."

The blonde security guard slinks past us, and the shaking
starts again. I can't believe it. Are they going to keep me?

Then I see it. My phone and passport, safe and sound in
Hollander's hands. She follows my gaze and nods. "I made
them give them back to me. You have every right to be here.
They kept saying it was fake."

"Look, Ms. Hollander, we said we were sorry," Meanie
says. "There have been a lot of fakes lately, and ICE has put

a high alert on certain countries and regions, especially areas like Kashmir. It's just protocol and we have to follow orders."

"Your protocol does not apply to a sixteen-year-old American citizen traveling alone."

"Yes, it does." Meanie's voice is firm, and he has a fake smile plastered to his face, which is now a livid red. "I don't make the rules. But I do follow them. And so should you, if you don't want to escalate this further."

The threat in his voice shuts Hollander right up, and I can't bring myself to open my mouth either. I just want to get out of here.

"Well, if everything is in order now, I think we should get moving," Hollander finally says. She takes my arm as the blonde brings my bag, which she's apparently repacked. "Check your stuff now, make sure you've got everything. Everyone's waiting."

"My mom—"

"Let's call her on the way to the gate," Hollander says. But I can't make myself move. What if they stop us again? What if they don't let me come back? I can see it now, all those years ahead of me, living in fear.

"Is there a problem, miss?" It's the blonde, her mouth still the same, disinterested, flat line. She literally could not care if I live or die.

I can't let her have the satisfaction.

"Yes," I say, using my best, take-no-prisoners debate voice. "We've got to hurry. We've got a flight to catch."

Hollander grabs my bag, and we race through the crowd toward the gate. "They're holding the flight," she says. "We have to be quick."

I hold fast to my boarding pass, passport and phone, unwilling to let them out of my sight again.

The man at the gate scans and lets us through immediately, his face concerned and apologetic.

And then we're on the plane, luggage stashed. Hollander takes a seat next to Andy, and nods toward the next row. "That's yours," she says. "Get settled." She pulls out her phone.

The empty seat is next to Rajan's. He stands, smiles, and hugs me really tight. I should be excited, but I still can't quite stop shaking. "Sorry you had to deal with that," he whispers into my hair. "It's happened to me before, too." He sighs. "Especially when I don't shave."

He stuffs my backpack under the seat, and Hollander leans across to pass me her phone. I can already hear my mom babbling at me in tearstained Hindi. My hands shake as I take it. "Beta, we were so worried. Ms. Hollander was so panicked. I thought—" My mom's voice breaks. "I thought—" I can hear her breathing hard, trying to get the words out. "Are you okay?"

I shake my head, even though she can't see me. "I'm on the plane now." My voice sounds far away, kind of like I left it that dark, cold room. "I'm not okay yet. But I will be."

I say goodbye and hang up as the flight attendant walks down the aisle, closing overhead bins, instructing passengers to buckle up.

I breathe in deep as we take off, watching as the earth sinks below us and we start to float above the clouds. And that's when I realize what's missing. My throat is bare, and it feels like everything's lost again.

"Oh," Rajan says, startling, reaching for his backpack. "I

grabbed this from the bin earlier. I didn't want you to forget it." He combs through the outside pocket and pulls out
a little tangle of gold.

And I've never been more grateful. For who I am. For who
I might get to be.

My Ganesh. The god of new beginnings.

ABOUT THE AUTHOR

The author of the YA doc dramedy *Symptoms of a Heartbreak*, SONA CHARAIPOTRA is not a doctor—much to her pediatrician parents' chagrin. They were really hoping she'd grow up to take over their practice one day. Instead, she became a writer, working as a celebrity reporter at *People* and (the dearly departed) *TeenPeople* magazines, and contributing to publications from the *New York Times* to *TeenVogue*. These days, she uses her master's in screenwriting from NYU and her MFA in creative writing from the New School to poke plot holes in her favorite teen TV shows, like *The Bold Type*—for work of course. She's the co-founder of CAKE Literary, a boutique book packaging company with a decidedly diverse bent, and the co-author (with Dhonielle Clayton) of the YA dance drama duology, *Tiny Pretty Things* and *Shiny Broken Pieces*, soon to be a Netflix Original TV series. Forthcoming are the psychological thriller *The Rumor Game* (with Dhonielle Clayton) and the contemporary YA comedy *How Maya Got Fierce*. Find her on the web at SonaCharaipotra.com, or on Twitter @sona_c.

● ● ●

THE CURANDERA AND THE ALCHEMIST

Maria E. Andreu

● ● ●

The first snow falls on a Tuesday. Tuesday is the day I teach English as a Second Language classes, a deeply improbable thing for me to be doing for a bunch of reasons. Like, because I once needed ESL classes. Like, because ESL for people like me, and my mom, for the men in the group I teach…well, maybe it's a bit of a tiny bandage on a heavy bleed. It makes no sense, but I want to do it anyway. Which I never would have imagined the day Ms. Scofield roped me into it.

The day of the first snow, I'm on my way to the library carrying my favorite book. The snow's tinkly magic lights the orange–blue sky and makes the whole world hold its breath. But, like all held breath, I should have known the moment couldn't last for long.

• • •

It is two months before the first-snow Tuesday. The intercom crackles to life. "Luisa Diaz, please come to Ms. Scofield's room."

Crap.

I check the time on my phone. Oh, not good. I had wandered into the library at the start of my free period. I meandered over to this dark part of the stacks in a blind corner where a bulb has gone out. I ran my finger over the spines slowly, willing them to speak to me. One did, its dark green cloth alive with promise. *The Alchemist's Confession.* From a glimpse at the author's name, I could tell it was mis-shelved. Maybe someone stashed it here so no one would find it. Or maybe they wanted only a certain kind of someone to find it, the kind of someone who gets lost in the dark nooks of libraries.

I turned to its first page.

It is the rare person who can withstand transformation, although so many think to wish it. Magic should be summoned only by the hardiest among us. I tried to explain this to her, but I loved her too dearly to do a good job of it. That's why things happened as they did.

Questions pricked at me, and soon I was tearing through page after page.

Now that the intercom has broken the spell, my phone tells me that I not only burned through my free period, but the one after that, gym. Maybe that's why Ms. Scofield—the school counselor—is calling me: detention for cutting class.

I pull the book up to my nose, an old habit. It smells faintly of old ink, of paper that was once too close to moisture and… something else. My mind hunts for the memory, but it escapes me.

One more minute. I'll go to Scofield's in a minute. The hunt for the memory the book's smell evokes takes me down blind alleys and lands me almost eight years ago, in the faraway village where my mother grew up.

● ● ●

When I was ten years old, the women of Colinas went across the street from my grandmother's house to see Don Isidro, the local curandero, one by one. They came back pale, clutching sweater fronts together with one hand near the neck and looking behind them, as if haunted. They whispered of being shown to the back room, where Don Isidro stayed when he came to visit. In a rustle of skirts and sisters they told the tale of what he'd said to them. "He's no good, just like I thought, he's running around," and, "Three branches from the willow, braid them together and…"

Inevitably someone would describe in detail what Don Isidro did during her top-secret visit, although the others reminded her she wasn't supposed to. He took a long puff of a big cigar and blew the smoke into a teacup, watched the pattern as it rose, then read a candle like it had her life story written in the flame in a way that sent her into uncontrollable shivers.

They shooed me away when they noticed I was listening. These were predictions and prescriptions I wasn't allowed to hear.

We were there in my mother's "back home" for six months. Long enough for Don Isidro to visit Colinas twice, once with enough time to see my mother. His visits were prized, and time with him was allotted by some unwritten math that only my aunts seemed to understand.

When I asked my mother what the curandero said, she replied, "He says we'll cross the border on a Tuesday. And that we'll make it through." That was all she'd tell me, although I could tell there was more. Maybe something about my father who'd died when I was little. A message, perhaps. That night I dreamed of sneaking to see Don Isidro myself. In my dream, I crawled into a teacup and floated in smoke, up, up, out of the cottage and following the spines of the mountains all the way to North America.

I resented being excluded from my mother's solo visit to the gnarled old cottage where the curandero's mother lived. Don Isidro came to stay with his blind, ancient mother every once in a while as part of his rounds. No one quite knew how far afield his rounds took him, but the news of his arrival back in town spread like wildfire through the dry brush at the foot of the cordillera. By the afternoon of the day he'd arrived, he was completely booked for his whole weeklong stay. Everyone went to him with a covered head and a basket of fruit, bills carefully folded in an envelope tucked in a pocket like he was some priest in a cathedral for dark spirits, not a dude in a ramshackle cottage by a canal running with icy water from the mountains.

Although the whole fuss about him was irritating, I was grateful for my mother's buoyed spirits after her visit to him. She had looked defeated for weeks at that point, like we'd never get back to the United States. Which was crazy, because the US was home. I'd gone to the States as a baby with my mother and grown up on Nickelodeon and Five Guys. When my mother picked me up from school in fifth grade and said, abruptly, "We need to go back home," it had taken me a long beat before I understood she meant the country she'd grown up in, not our basement apartment. "Abuela's sick. We have to go."

Once we'd gone, we'd been stuck there. Stuck as my grandmother grew skinny in a matter of weeks, as my mother and my aunts washed her, faces lined with purpose. Stuck as everyone shuffled in wearing black and wailed in the front room with the big TV that looked like it was from the 1950s, and which had long been repurposed into a display case for knick-knacks. Stuck after that, too, while the sisters decided what to do with the house, hinting it was time for us to go so the mud-walled place could be sold.

Stuck when we couldn't get a visa to come back to the US because we'd overstayed our last one.

My mother had tried bribes and long lines, but we didn't get a visa. She signed away her rights to her share of her mother's house for enough money for us to take a plane to Mexico and then paid a guy to smuggle us in. On the US side the guy who'd led us across stuck us in a room with peeling wallpaper and told my mother he wouldn't let us out until we paid him more. But he did let us out.

I never did find out how my mother paid what he asked for, because by that point all she had was a ten-dollar bill in a fake pocket she'd sewn into her bra.

● ● ●

I shake the memory away. Scofield is definitely going to give me a detention. But it might just be worth it. The book was so engrossing, the descriptions so alive and intoxicating, that it was as if it had bewitched me to keep reading. An alchemist is not a curandero, but there were similarities between the book and my memories of Don Isidro. Maybe it wasn't the smell that reminded me of my mother's visit to Don Isidro, but the magical ether that seemed to run through the two things.

They were the same, the alchemist from the book and old Don Isidro, in ways I couldn't identify on a test, in ways I felt somewhere behind my throat. But not entirely. The alchemist falls in love with a showgirl and creates the most magical theater in all of London, where people for hundreds of miles come to be mesmerized and amazed, just like the women of my mother's town were amazed. Who knows what Don Isidro was up to, why he left and roamed and came back unexpectedly. Maybe he ran a secret magical theater too.

I pull myself up off the library floor, take out my ponytail, and scrape my hair back with ragged nails into what I hope is a semblance of a respectable, visit-the-school-counselor look, then put my ponytail back in. Teachers and counselors never get tired of telling you not to judge a book by its cover, but that's basically all they do, reading the superficial tea leaves of absences or rumor to figure out who to haul down to the office. As if they could know any of us in the hundreds of faces they deal with every day. I bet she has a checklist. I'm stressing it, but she just got to the Ds and that's why she called me in.

Although probably not.

Ms. Scofield's office is two doors away from the main office. I know there's no reason for the actual office to make me nervous, but it does. And so does being this close to it. I knock on her door gently.

"Luisa, is that you?" I hear through the thin, plastic-y wood. I turn the knob, open the door. "Hi, Ms. Scofield."

"Thank you so much for coming. Come in, come in." She moves her hand like she's fanning herself.

She thanks me as if I could have just told the school counselor I wasn't coming.

I sit in the chair across from her. Her office is like a hospital gift shop: fake cheer abounds. You never go to the school counselor when you're happy, but the room is floor-to-ceiling motivational posters, bright boxes, hot-pink feather boas and, as if that wasn't weird enough, a frog puppet inside a frog basket that looks more appropriate for a kindergarten than a high school. She pulls an iPad off a table that's covered with magazines and bits of what look like colored index cards. She swipes at it languidly, without a lot of commitment. Its brightness glints off her glasses.

"Well, your SATs were stellar. Really good work there. You were in the top four percent of the school, and even better statewide. Your grades, though. Talk to me about that."

"I…uh." I leave it at that. She's going to have to ask a better question. Or give me time to come up with a better answer. My throat is full of things I want to hold and not say. To explain it to her would require so much backstory. It would be like asking someone to read a book before teaching them the alphabet. Just the thought of trying makes me want to curl into a ball.

"Top of your class freshman and sophomore years. Pretty good the first half of junior year. So you can obviously do the work. And then the second part of junior year and here at the start of senior year you're in…well, I was going to say 'free fall,' but that's not very counselor-y, is it?" She actually winks. She's not very old, so I guess she thinks she can still get away with the I'm-not-like-all-these-other-oldsters-who-just-don't-get-it stance.

"I guess *free fall* is a fair term," I say. I'm not going to make it easy for her. Some part of me thinks it's her job to see more.

"Your attendance is not great either," she says. I guess I should appreciate the fact that she's being straight. I do not. I run my nails over the rough fabric of the sides of the chair. Her solutions to my attendance problems will probably involve watching videos and writing essays. I need a lawyer. Not even that. New laws. A magic wand.

I keep my gaze on the space just above where her eyebrows meet. I read somewhere that people think you're looking in their eyes when you do that.

She puts the iPad down. "Is there anything you want to talk about? How are things at home?"

"Fine."

She nods her slow I-know-what's-up nod. I saw it during junior year, when my grades first started slipping and she called me in. I wonder if she remembers. She's acting like this is the first time we've talked about this.

"I spoke to a few of your teachers. Their sense is that you've lost your motivation. We have a creative solution for you. If you're open to hearing it."

I slide up the chair a little. Creative solutions aren't going to fix my problem. But they're like a scent I can't ignore, and I let myself listen even through the ammonia smell of what's-the-use. So the deal is this: come here, to the public library, Tuesday nights, teach ESL, and they'll count it as an independent study, which can supplement either my English grade or my history grade. I have no idea what ESL class has to do with history, but maybe they picked the two classes I'm most sucking wind in and organized it with those teachers. I'm not sure how this is even okay by the rules, but it was their idea. I know some of my classmates have hustled Senior Independent Instruction Programs—SIIPs—for senior year. Like Amanda from my math class is supposed to be helping to file at her mother's law firm, but I know for a fact she goes to the mall and her mother's law clerk signs the slips so that the school doesn't get wise to her. I wanted to do one, but I had no idea where I could get an Independent Study gig, so I didn't even try.

ESL is on the second floor, at a set of light wood tables set up next to an enormous circle window through which you can see the town hall and the leaves turning showy shades of yellow and red, and some going straight to brown. I know how you feel, brown trees. It seems a lot of work to turn something gorgeous only to have it all fall off and get carted away in big yellow garbage trucks.

The woman who runs ESL looks like she started working here roughly around the time George Washington got inaugurated. She's all wispy white hair and powder-blue sweater pulled primly over bones and old boobs. She greets me as I walk through the door.

"Jennifer called and said you'd be coming. Do you have any experience teaching ESL?"

"I speak Spanish," I answer. It's weird to hear her calling Ms. Scofield by her first name.

She regards me through sharp blue eyes. "That's too bad," she says. "Slows it down, actually, if you speak their native language. Although a few of the day laborers speak Mam and K'iche'. Don't suppose you speak either of those, do you? It's good to hold most of the class in English, but we're in desperate need of some way to communicate basic things in Mam and K'iche'."

"I…no." I don't tell her I'm not even sure what those are.

She turns away, leading me toward a table. "That's too bad," she says again. I appear to be a deep disappointment to her even though we've only just met. She gives me a stack of photocopied pages from a book. "I'm Betsy, by the way," she says.

I am tempted to answer, *Ross?* But I don't.

My first student is a man named Florencio who sits across from me looking nervous. I use the word *man* loosely, because he looks nearly as young as I am, and he's slight. His hands are rough, full of scars and with a dry patch on each index finger. Betsy tells me most of the students who come to learn English at the library are the same guys who wait for work by the overpass near the highway that runs through the next town over. But I have a hard time squaring that with Florencio's dark blue jeans with the white stitching and his fresh haircut, which looks just like the one a bunch of the guys in my school have—short on the sides, spiky in front. I squint at him to make sure I don't actually know him from school. This seems to make him more nervous.

"Hello, Florencio," I say, following Betsy's instructions to speak to the students only in English. "I am Luisa."

He smiles and nods. He looks unsure.

"Have you done any ESL classes before?"

He smiles nervously, his eyes blank.

I side-eye Betsy. She's sitting down with a student several

tables away, and there are three other tutor-student pairs between me and her.

I drop my voice lower and ask again, this time in Spanish. Hearing me speak a language he understands makes Florencio's eyes light up, and he raises his voice an octave as he responds. This is his first ESL class. He arrived in the US only two months ago. He is staying with his cousin, and he already has a full-time job working for a landscaper. I want to ask him how old he is, but he doesn't volunteer the information, and it seems rude to ask.

I quickly switch back to the sheet that Betsy gave me. Introduction Games, it says. I skim the instructions and realize it's an activity for a large group. I flip to the next one. It's called Name Game. It's also for a group, but I think Florencio and I can pull this off. I explain the rules to him. I cheat and explain them in Spanish, but insist we do the game in English.

"I'll start," I say. "My name is Luisa and I like to read books."

He smiles. "Me name is Florencio," he says, sounding each syllable out slowly. "I like me home."

"That's good," I said. "But what do you like to do?"

"I like me home," he repeats, his grin wide and earnest.

• • •

Tuesday nights become part of my routine. Fall progresses, and soon I can't see the trees through the big, round window, because it's dark even when we start. I shift from T-shirts and cut-up jeans to bulky sweaters and tights under my pants. Florencio comes every week with his sheet filled out, his homework done as if I have the power to fail him, or even grade him. I am humbled by the responsibility. I try to make the connection—if he's trying so hard, maybe I should try too. One day he shows up with a black eye, but when I ask about it, he mutters something about a lawn mower and raps his knuckle on the handout to change the subject.

He learns quickly. He misses some classes, and when he does, I sit with another student. The following week he apologizes and explains that his work ran late, too late for English class. Although I teach others, none have Florencio's ease with the language, the delight that sparkles in his eyes when he understands a hard-to-translate saying or makes a connection to something he learned before. He tells me stories about deciphering billboards and understanding an entire interview on the radio his boss was playing in the truck on the way to a job.

"Ahora tu," he says, then catches himself. "You story."

I let my mind wander over the events of my week. Amanda having a fight with Josh in the hall. Ms. Scofield calling me in for a progress meeting. It all feels impossibly small, not a thing worth his invitation.

Instead, I tell him the story of the curandero, how he knew we'd cross the border on a Tuesday. Florencio's eyes get wide and serious. "Magic is real," he says. Then he lets himself slip into Spanish to say, "Some people can touch it easier than others."

In November, Ms. Scofield sits with me and picks out a list of colleges to which I should apply. My grades haven't gotten better, but she says I can supplement my application with the volunteer work I'm doing, highlight my SAT scores and explain my extenuating circumstances. She lets that hang there, the only time she's ever nodded at the elephant in the corner. I want to shake her, shake the optimism right out of her, the deeply American way she believes, in her marrow, that everything can work out. She doesn't understand that it doesn't always work out, not for people like me, not for the men at ESL, not for Florencio. She doesn't get that grades don't matter when you don't have nine simple digits to write on your applications, when your passport is the wrong color, when you're not eligible for in-state tuition or scholarships or loans, when your mother cleans hotel rooms for a living, which doesn't leave a lot for books and board.

I don't say any of these things. I take her printed list and fold it neatly before putting it in my pocket. I'll throw it away in the hall when I'm out of sight.

• • •

Florencio gets bored with Betsy's exercises. I tell him to bring a book he'd like to learn to read. The next week he shows up with a small black book with a black plastic cover. New American Bible. I want to tell him I meant that he should bring a story, but when he begins to read hesitantly from the tiny type on the onionskin paper, a peaceful glow comes over him, and I feel sheepish that I almost complained about his choice of reading. We work through several weeks of this until he says, "Next week, you bring book."

The first snow has carpeted the streets the following Tuesday. I make my way to the public library slowly, enjoying the muffled stillness, the sparkles under the streetlights. The snow is showing off, reminding me of its arresting beauty. I look up and watch it glimmer on its way down. It sprinkles my cheeks and instantly melts into me, into every other time it's drifted down to make me feel alive, like wonders still happen.

The library door opens with a whoosh, and inside all the

crinkling magic dissipates in the recycled air. I've brought my school's copy of *The Alchemist's Confession*. The passage I want to read with Florencio, one of my favorites, is bookmarked with a piece of composition notebook paper.

I walk up to the second floor. The space is heavy, funereal. Have I come on the wrong day? All the volunteers are there. Betsy is crying, tears streaming down her face with no sound.

"Where is everyone?" I ask. They look at each other, and no one says anything.

Finally Betsy speaks up. "There was an ICE raid. They hit several companies in the area. Got a lot of our guys. A few are okay, but they're afraid to come."

"Florencio?" I ask, my hand tightening around the green cover of the book I'd brought to share with him.

Betsy's face crumples. "I'm sorry, Luisa. I'm so sorry."

• • •

I don't go to school the next day, or the one after that. I've turned eighteen, and they can't make me. My mother leaves for work too early to know.

I know it is only a matter of time before what happened to Florencio happens to me too. A cop will ask me for identification, maybe, or I'll try to get a job under the table and, without the right papers, I'll get found out. And if not me, then my mother. So instead I will melt into this bed, a creaky little cot my mother bought secondhand at the Salvation Army when we found our next place after the basement. It folds in half for easy storage, although we never store it. I imagine it has magical powers and I can fold it with me in it, and it will take me someplace better. Like the smoke from the old dream, maybe.

My mother comes home from work mad. The school has gotten through to her and reported my absences. I try to explain about the senselessness of all of it, but she doesn't understand either. She's hopeful too, not American every-problem-has-a-solution hopeful, but I've-seen-worse hopeful. "We came here to succeed, not to stay in bed. Work or study, but stay home? No," she says. It is as stern as I've ever heard her.

• • •

The next time I can bring myself to go to ESL, I find out from Betsy how to get in to see Florencio in immigration detention. I don't tell my mother I'm going, because she'd burst into flames if I told her I was going to a jail, a place where I have to show ID to be allowed in, a place where they could just as easily open the doors and put me in for the same exact reason Florencio is in there. But I need to see him, and so I go.

He looks even smaller behind the thick yellowing glass partition that separates inmates and visitors. A flare of anger bursts through me as I see him in the orange jumpsuit, hands shackled together. They have him in a jail with people who have hurt people, who are dangerous. This man—this boy—who glows when he reads Genesis and thrills when he deciphers a new billboard does not belong here.

I sit across from him. "This is some bad luck," he says in Spanish, his face twisted into a half grin.

"That's an understatement," I say in English. He hasn't heard the word, and I do my best to explain it to him.

"Ah, that's a smart word. We don't have that word in Spanish. Estos se las saben todas." I laugh. It is a common immigrant's saying, something close to *Americans have it all figured out.*

"I don't know about that. They put you in here. They obviously don't know everything."

He waves his hand as best he can through his bindings. "Ah, don't worry so much about me. Remember what I told you the first day we had class?"

"That you liked home."

He nods. He continues in Spanish, "I came to earn money. My mother is getting old, and I wanted a better life for her. I didn't do everything I wanted to do, but I did something. I will be happy to see her."

I nod.

"You brought the book?" he asks.

I pull it out of the big inside pocket of my winter coat.

"This glass is dirty. I won't be able to read through it. You read it to me," he says.

I draw in a long, stilling breath. I close my eyes and try to find the peace I felt on the walk to the library through the snow, the moment in which silence and magic seemed to suspend everything else, the moment Florencio was already gone but I didn't yet know it. Maybe in that instant, things were good not just because I didn't know, but because everything was possible. Or because it was in the loss of Florencio, in the negative space he left, that I saw that trying is worth it, even when you're not quite sure why.

I begin reading from the marked page. "The alchemist said 'It's not magic, Hannah, not in the way you're thinking, in the sleight of hand, hocus-pocus way. Alchemy is not that. It is creating something fine of a baser thing. The alchemist desires nothing more than to make something new and un-expected out of materials no one knows are precious.'

"'I don't understand,' said Hannah, her lips a kiss between a ruby and a rose, 'Things are what they are,' she added, with more than a hint of petulance."

I stopped to explain a few words Florencio didn't know, like *petulance*. Then I resumed.

"Barnaby responded, 'Spoken like someone who believes only what is put in front of her. Alchemists don't look at what is, but what could be.' As he spoke, the bud rose in the lapel of his perfectly pressed suit jacket seemed to nod in approval.

"Hannah was bored by talk she couldn't understand. 'Yes, that's all well and good,' she said. 'But does that mean you'll build me a theater where I can be the grandest lady on the stage?' She shook her golden curls like little bells. She really could be quite winning."

The reading is slow. I have to stop and translate more words for Florencio.

"Barnaby laughed. 'We'll start there,' he said, the corners of his eyes creased with love. He wished he could explain that he wanted her to be a great lady because loving her would thus make him a great man. She looked about, smoothed a ruffle on her skirt. Her attention was already straying. He wouldn't try to explain. That was only half the truth, any-way. He wanted to build her dream, because he hoped to live in a world where dreams come true."

I put the book down. I look at Florencio, at the blocky letters stenciled on his prison uniform. His eyes are glowing much like they did when he read to me in the library. He looks down the line of others also pressing green old-timey phone receivers to their ears.

It takes him a long time, but he finally says something. "Luisa, no te preocupes por mi. You no worry. My dreams still coming. You build yours. Okay?"

I nod and tilt my head forward so that the tears can drop straight down into my lap.

EIGHT MONTHS LATER

On the first day of community college, the professor asks us to write an essay on our intended major. I have no idea what I want mine to be. Just because I've bought myself this one little step, it doesn't mean I have faith that I'll weave this strand into something that will pass all the tests I'll need to withstand. I still don't have papers. I am still trying to build something new out of the old, experiment by experiment, smoke in a teacup, wishes and lies. And I want to live in a world where people like me can become what they want to be.

I pull out a fresh sheet of loose leaf. Across the top I write, *Curandera crossed with Alchemist*. I'm not sure if I'll be able to make the professor understand why that's what I want to be, what I already am. But I will try.

ABOUT THE AUTHOR

MARIA E. ANDREU crossed the Mexican border into the US undocumented at the age of eight. She "got her papers" at eighteen, and did her best to forget all about that. But as her pursuit of finding the right words in her inscrutable adopted language led to a dream of being a writer, she found that the stories that most clamored to be told were those of feeling excluded, of what it means to belong, of who gets to say "Come on in." Her debut novel, *The Secret Side of Empty*, is the story of an undocumented teen girl. Maria's work has also appeared in *Teen Vogue*, *Newsweek* and the *Washington Post*. Her forthcoming novel is about what it's like to be new in the United States, and to ache to find the right words to say all that's in your heart.

A BIGGER TENT

Maurene Goo

To my family and our little tent.

There's this really TMI Korean saying: if you laugh while crying, a hair will grow out of your butt.

I didn't realize that talking about butt hair was kind of gross until I was older. Me, at some slumber party, probably: "What? Don't all your families casually talk about butt hair?"

Sometimes it takes being away from your family to realize what a pack of weirdos they are.

I looked out the window as my plane descended into LA and felt a familiar knot of dread tighten in my chest. My body was bracing itself for seeing them.

After spending two months in London, viewing LA from high above was truly depressing. Thick, beige smog cloaked the city, which sprawled out between giant mountains and the ocean. Buildings dotted the landscape forever and ever.

It never ended. No one in LA knew what was actually a part of LA. You just knew when you weren't in it anymore.

When I left customs, I turned on my phone and was hit with a billion unread texts from my mom.

Text us when you land!

Okay looks like your flight is on time.

Maybe a little early. We'll leave a little early, too, just in case.

Dad says he'll wait in the parking garage and then come out when you text him.

Nevermind we are all coming now.

I blew out an agitated breath. Of course they were.

We are here! No rush, just text when you are done.

No rush. Just texting you again to passive-aggressively re-mind you to rush!

We're by baggage claim now.

I gripped my carry-on handle as I rolled it through a dingy corridor. Once, it had probably been really sleek and mod-ern, but now it was just neglected and worn out. The fluores-cent lights flickered overhead. LAX was such a pit. I thought back to the impeccably designed spaces of Heathrow. Why did anyone live in the US?

Two months had flown by. My summer academic program in London had been a dream. After winning an essay contest,

I'd been invited to study engineering for free at some random fancy British high school. It was the best summer of my life. Everything but flights were covered, and my parents had let me stay an extra month.

"Aren't you homesick?" my older brother Ron would ask from his dorm room at UC Irvine. Orange County was the farthest Ron would live. He drove the hour home most weekends so that my mom could do his laundry for him.

No, I hadn't been homesick. In fact, the second I'd arrived in London, I had felt so grounded, so assured. I was able to be a version of myself that I'd known was in there—buried under sixteen years with my family.

"Nari-yah!"

Hearing my Korean name yelled out in public was always startling. But there was my mom, waving her arms frantically, like she was hoping for a helicopter rescue on a desert island. Ron and Dad were next to her.

A claustrophobic trio of good intentions.

My dad clapped me on the shoulder. "You look skinny."

"Because bad British food, huh?" my mom said, looking at me with a furrowed brow. She was doing the Korean Mom Body Scan: skin too tan, hair unbrushed, approximately 3.25 pounds lost.

My brother grunted a hello. Right. This was my family. I thought of how I'd cried and hugged every single friend in my fellowship program my last day in London. Generous in my feelings.

"I love you guys," I had said while weeping. It was so easy to say.

I missed them already.

When we got home, all I wanted to do was to crash in my bed and sleep for a week. But my parents had other plans.

"Everyone's coming over tonight," my dad said as he turned on the TV, the sound blaring through the house.

"Oh, my God," I hollered over the noise. "Can we not? I'm so tired."

"It's okay, you can just eat and go to sleep," my mom said.

But that was never going to happen. That evening, extended family members stuffed themselves into the one-story ranch house. I was happy to see my cousins, as close to me as siblings. Their noisy company kept my jet lag at bay.

"Nari Unni, were the guys in London cute?" My cousin Rachel slumped into a giant pillow in our family room and wagged her eyebrows at me. She was fourteen, obsessed with K-pop boys, and her horniness had no bounds.

I laughed. "So cute. They dress really nicely there."

"Better than me?" Rachel's twin brother Daniel kept his eyes on the video game he was playing.

"Better than a T-shirt with a dragon wearing sunglasses and the words *Summer Is Coming* underneath? Yeah, somehow they've surpassed your level."

Ron held the other controller. They were in some medieval landscape filled with white-people elves and mossy ruins. "Nari thinks everything in London was better than here. She's so worldly now."

"Shut up." I frowned. "When you guys leave here—if you ever leave here, Ronald—then you'll know, too. The world is big." And I was ready for it.

"It's not like we live in some podunk town," Ron said as his character shot an arrow into a troll thing. "You live in a place that other people dream of living in, too, you know."

"Yeah, actors."

Dinner was well-orchestrated chaos. After years of dining together, everyone knew when to reach for the banchan— the little side dishes—and when to dip their spoon into the communal bowls of soup.

Living with a bunch of Europeans, I'd had to adjust to a lot of new table manners. With my family, there was no *Can you please pass the salt?* Life was too short for that. You ate when you could, no offense taken when your uncle almost elbowed you in the face to get to the blanched spinach.

"Mom, remember when you made this soup on that one camping trip?" Ron said after he shoveled a huge spoonful into his mouth.

She nodded as she flitted around the table, refilling side dishes, checking on everyone's rice bowls. When they hosted dinner, my parents never sat down; there was too much to do in the kitchen. They ate when everyone else had finished.

"That camping trip was such a long time ago. What, three years?" said my oldest uncle from my dad's side.

"A long time," one of my aunts said with a nod. "The kids don't want to do trips like that anymore."

"That's not true," Ron protested. "I love camping."

"Me too," said Rachel.

The little kid table piped up with "Yeah!"

"Camping!"

Oh no.

My dad sat up, excitement thrumming through him with big chihuahua energy. "Let's do it! The kids don't start school for another couple weeks!"

I tried to make eye contact with my cousins. Like, let us

thwart this while we can. But everyone was into it except for me. And by the end of dinner, we had a plan.

I slept for thirteen hours that night.

• • •

One week later, we were, indeed, headed on a camping trip.

"We're still using that tent?" I asked, pointing at the orange nylon bundle covered in a fine coat of dirt.

My dad shoved a beach chair into the trunk next to the tent. "Yeah!"

"Dad. It's tiny."

"We still fit into it," he said, his voice strained as he maneuvered the cooler in.

"Barely! You got that tent when we were little kids. Don't you think it's time to upgrade?"

"Why buy something new when this works perfectly fine?"

The eternal question.

Ron came out of the house with a hard-shell rolling suitcase.

"What in the world is that?" I asked.

"Mom's stuff," he said, handing it to my dad.

"Why is she bringing luggage camping?! Where's the backpack we got her last year?"

Ron shrugged. "I don't know. She said this was more durable."

"No one brings a freaking suitcase camping."

"Well, I guess we do," he said as he went back inside for more stuff.

I was only a baby when our family immigrated to LA from Seoul. Ron was three. It seemed like those three years were pivotal in our hardwiring or something. All our lives he had never been as baffled or frustrated as I'd been with our parents. He'd never gotten in trouble for sneaking out to a party. When he was in high school, Ron and his weirdo friends spent weekends watching Tom Cruise movies and playing music in the garage. He had absolutely no desire to go on snowboarding trips up to Big Bear or to a school dance.

Watching my sturdy father wrestle with my mom's suitcase made me feel a melancholy deep in my soul. This camping trip was the highlight of his year. My dad worked long, tedious hours as an insurance broker and he never took vacation days. It was admirable, I guess, but also annoying. Everyone else takes vacation days, just take yours, Dad! No one was handing out extra credit for killing yourself at work.

We hit the road, pretty much spilling out of the car. I rested on a sleeping bag wedged between my head and the window, willing myself into a coma until we got there.

"Hook me up to the Bluetooth." Ron jostled me as he leaned forward, popping his head between my parents in the front.

I shook my head. "No. Don't play that EDM crap."

"Rude," he said with a jab into my side. "Why do you care? You're going to be passed out the entire ride."

"I won't if you play that garbáge," I said, using a French accent.

"Stop speaking French. You sound like a douche."

"Ron. That wasn't French. In fact, 'douche' is French. God, read a book."

"Oh, I'm gonna learn French from reading books?"

I was about to kick him in the shin when my dad honked the horn, startling all of us.

"Are you going to be babies on this entire ride?" my dad barked, waving his hand in the air with a quick karate chop. "Shameful. How old are you?"

I closed my eyes. "I'm still a teenager. Ron's a loser super senior."

Ron's head swiveled. "How in the world did you become more of a bitch in London? I didn't think it was humanly possible."

My mom smacked his head so fast that her hand was a flesh-colored blur. "Yah!"

He blinked. "I'm too old for this."

I slept the rest of the drive and woke up only when the car slowed, the tires crunching on unpaved road.

● ● ●

The campsite was nestled into a national park with a desert landscape. We had caravanned with two other extended families, and unpacking was a chaotic flurry that involved a lot of transactions in the oppressive heat.

"Who has an extra sleeping bag?"

"We have blankets!"

"Okay, we'll take those."

I stared at my aunts as they passed a giant floral-print comforter to each other. "Why didn't you realize you were short a sleeping bag?" I asked, my voice flat.

"We did. But I knew someone would have something extra!" my aunt responded as she walked briskly toward her tent.

"Are you going to stand there with your commentary or actually help?" my uncle barked as he walked by me with a giant cooler.

Why we'd decided to come to the one campground in the

state not up in the mountains was beyond me. This was an arid wasteland full of chaparral, spindly pine trees, and craggy boulders. In the summer, everything in Southern California was a desiccated hellscape. I remembered the rolling green hills of the English countryside. How everything was just so happy to be there. Blossoming and unfurling itself to the beauty of its surroundings.

I made a face at my uncle and dragged myself to our tiny tent, where my mom was inside, kneeled over and cleaning the tent floor with a wet rag. Cleaning up once we set up camp was the first activity all the women in my family did. One of my aunts had even brought her cordless vacuum to pass around to everyone.

It annoyed me that they cared about how clean the tents were, but it annoyed me more that only the women cared.

"Mom. It's going to get dirty in five minutes."

"So? We mess up our beds every night, does this mean we shouldn't make our beds?" She blew a strand of hair away from her face as she swept the rag around.

Who could argue with that airtight logic?

I squinted into the tent. "We're going to be squished in here. I can sleep in the car."

"The car?" My mom looked at me as if I had suggested killing a human being for dinner. "Don't be cray-jee."

So many things were cray-jee to my mom. Shaving my legs for the first time. Borrowing clothes from my friends. Sleeping with the fan on. Cray-jee.

But there was no way I was spending the weekend sleeping in that tiny thing with my entire family, their proximity suffocating me, minute by minute, snore by snore.

● ● ●

After everyone unpacked, Ron discovered a little body of water near the campsite. Excited, we took off our dusty shoes and waded in. It was barely a pond, but it was cool and in one of the few shaded areas of the campgrounds.

The moms sat in their hodgepodge collection of folding chairs in the shade. Our family had brought an old pink beach chair that usually sat rusting in the garage. The sight of that chair agitated me. Why didn't we just get camping chairs? And why did we have only one chair? It was always a free-for-all scramble in the evening, when everyone wanted to sit in an actual chair. Most of us ended up balancing our asses on pointy rocks or perched on the edge of a cooler. If I tried to take a chair, my mom would throw me a dirty look so that I would give it up to an aunt or uncle.

She looked happy in her giant sun hat, her trim ankles crossed as she fanned herself with a paper plate. I rarely got to see her relaxed. I could count the number of actual vacations we'd been on as a family with one hand. And even then, she was always bouncing from one task to another, never actually able to enjoy the moment.

Sometimes I wondered what the point of all of this was for my parents. Leaving their home to go to a foreign country where they were constantly playing catch-up. Where every choice, every moment lived, was an investment in their children. An investment that I was sure I would never pay off for them.

"Ouch!" I heard Rachel screech. "I'm getting eaten alive by mosquitoes!"

My head snapped up. Mosquitoes were my sworn enemy. One bite kept me swollen and itchy for days. One by one, everyone in the pond starting screeching and swatting at themselves. I felt it, too, then. A sting on my forearm. Then on my forehead. On my neck.

We left the pond screaming and slapping our skin.

• • •

My parents wouldn't let me sleep in the car that night.

I tossed and turned between the edge of the tent and my mom. My face grazed the nylon. God damn it. I reached above my head for the netted pocket, feeling around for my phone.

It was only 10:00 p.m.

There was absolutely nothing to do at night when you camp but sleep. I was in for a long night.

I had a single bar of cell phone service. With the patience of a monk, I waited as Instagram loaded. Had anyone commented on my photo of last night's sunset? I had managed to document this camping trip in the most interesting way I could. *Cali does sunsets right.*

My story feed was full of images from the London crew. Boomerangs of frosty beer glasses clinking each other. The city lights diffused by fog and rain. Videos that were indecipherable with everyone's laughter distorting the audio.

I watched them late into the night.

• • •

The next day started off with a hike. It was a million degrees already despite it being fairly early. I covered my head with a lightweight jacket to shield my scalp from the relentless sun.

One of my aunts walked beside me, pumping her arms enthusiastically. Depressing that my middle-aged aunt was in better shape than me. She nudged me. "Did you have fun in London, Nari?"

I nodded, my feet picking up to match her pace. "Yeah, it was really fun." Fun didn't begin to explain it. When I had met up with my friends in LA, there weren't enough words to describe my time there. But with my family, I just couldn't get them out. I wasn't able to be myself with them, lately.

"It better have been more than fun," my mom muttered as she walked up to us. "It cost a fortune."

Guilt seeped through me. Slow and sludgy. While the travel and lodging had been covered by the scholarship, my parents had paid for the extra month that I stayed there. They had even given me some money to travel a bit.

It's not that I didn't feel gratitude. I just didn't like how I was supposed to be performative of this gratitude. Resentment now filled the spaces where I had only felt thankful and content.

There was just so much bullshit wrapped up in being a good immigrant kid.

So I set my jaw stubbornly and shrugged. "Not everything is measured by money, Mom."

That made everyone laugh, but my mom flashed me a warning look. "Don't talk back."

Normally that would have me biting my tongue, not wanting to deal with Mom wrath. But it was hot. And I was irritated. And I hated this camping trip.

"Don't be annoying, then." A hush came over everyone walking near us. A heat that had nothing to do with the temperature flooded my face.

"What?" Mom's voice was basically death.

I walked faster but my mom kept up with me. "I'm so sick of this trip."

"We never should have sent you to London!" my mom shouted. "Ever since you've been back, you've been acting like a little ingrate! Do you think you're better than your family?!"

Family members were bolting as far as they could from us. I turned around, then. "Yeah, I do! I can't wait to just leave." Before I sprinted off the trail, I got one last look at my mom's face. The disappointment sucked all the air out of my lungs.

• • •

My feet crunched through leaves. Somehow, I'd ended up alone in a wooded area. We had climbed in altitude and it was cooler here. The sun was setting and the bugs were coming out. Shit. I wished my exposed limbs could shrink into my body.

It was fine. I was fine. I wasn't a little kid. I would find the trail again.

Um...what was it that Bear Grylls always did? Look for a water source? Where there was water there was a trail? And then a trail led to a road. Which led to civilization. Right.

I stood stock-still, hoping to hear water. But why would there be water when we'd been hauling ass on these horrible switchbacks for hours? We had been walking straight up a mountain. But I was in the woods. There was water in the woods, right?

Suddenly all my knowledge about planet Earth disappeared from my brain. What even were mountains? Why were woods? Oh God, I was going to die on a camping trip with my dumb family.

I had stormed off so long ago that I had no idea when I'd

stopped hearing their voices. The chatter that had made me shove AirPods in my ears had been replaced by ominous forest noises. Crunching leaves. An owl hoot. Owls were freaky, okay?

It was so late that I couldn't see where the sun was setting in the sky, which would have oriented me. The sun set in the west, right?

Who cares if you know where west is? It's not like you looked at a freaking map before hitting this trail. Get your head together!

I took a deep breath and tried to retrace my steps. But here's the thing about trees: THEY ALL LOOK ALIKE. For about five minutes I tried to memorize the distinct quality of certain trees until I realized that distinguishing them now was absolutely worthless.

When the air was metallic with cold and my eyes strained to see in the dark, I started to cry. Crap. Suddenly, I didn't feel like someone who was ready to leave home and start college.

I felt like a lost little kid.

Completely alone. Without the cocoon that was always there—suffocating, yes, but warm, too. Protective. I sat down on a felled oak tree and rubbed my arms for warmth, tears stinging my eyes. I feared death by bear, but mostly I feared the loneliness.

Who knew if it was seconds or minutes or hours that ticked by—but suddenly I heard a voice and saw a beam of light. A flashlight.

I stood up and started yelling. "HERE! I'm here!"

The voices grew closer, the lights brighter, and then suddenly I was surrounded by rangers and my family. Relief seared through me and I let my mom hug me, hard and fierce.

"You almost killed me," she said, her voice high-pitched and furious.

My face was crushed into her shoulder. "I know. Sorry." And I think she knew what I meant. That was the thing with my family. We didn't talk about our feelings because, sometimes, it was completely unnecessary. Our emotions were plugged into each other, for better or worse.

• • •

The next morning, after a night of relieved eating and campfire dumbassery, our tent was shaking so hard even Ron woke up early.

When I opened the tent flap, a wall of dust whooshed by. I closed my eyes and tried to zip the flap shut. "Oh, my God. It's so windy."

My mom gasped. "Oh no, we left a lot of stuff out!" She started to scramble out of her sleeping bag, knocking into everyone. My dad turned to his side and continued to sleep.

I resisted the urge to be annoyed by my mom's overreaction and instead said, "I'll help you." My mom paused and looked at me, satisfaction flickering across her features.

Ron plopped back into his sleeping back. I kicked him. "If I'm getting up, you are too." He grabbed my ankle with older-brother speed and I fell over, slamming my elbows into him. My dad woke up at that point.

A few minutes later we were all outside, bleary-eyed and covering our faces with our sweatshirts as the wind continued to kick up dirt.

My family members were scrambling—grabbing chairs

that were knocked over, stuffing paper plates and cups into coolers, picking up errant jackets and boots.

The wind didn't let up all day. Our usual breakfast of ramen cooked with egg was nixed because the portable stove couldn't keep a flame. We decided to head back home a day early, and I was relieved. We were the last family to get our stuff together, and we agreed to meet our relatives at the nearest Denny's.

While loading the trunk, with our tent half packed up, the wind got brutal, and I dove into our car. Everyone else in my family seemed to have the same idea. One by one, they opened the doors and joined me.

"Wow, this is so exciting huh?" my dad said, slapping his hands on the steering wheel. Any force of nature excited my father. Needing to use survival skills gave him life. He loved going to Costco to stock up on "rations," getting sandbags from the fire department, handing out flashlights. I felt a genuine gladness for him then. That he was able to have this moment on his camping trip.

My mom's brow furrowed. "There's going to be dirt in all of our stuff." An eternity-long list of worries was no doubt unrolling in her mind.

But before she could start spiraling, Ron tapped his hand on the window. "Wait. Is our tent...moving?"

I glanced out at the orange blob. It was, in fact, moving. One of the corners was pivoting—the stake must have come out.

"Omo." My mom gasped.

Another stake came out. The tent was tilting to one side now.

"Uh-oh," I said.

We all bolted out of the car. But before any of us could reach the tent, it was lifted high up into the air in one jerky movement.

"Um." Ron froze next to me.

The tent was flying.

A small orange dome, levitating as flurries of leaves swirled around it. Bouncing gently from left to right. Moving a little higher with each passing second.

We were standing in a line, heads tilted back. Quiet as we watched the tent get swept up higher and higher.

The sky was bright blue and endless. That scrap of orange had so much freedom now. It wasn't tethered by flimsy stakes. Filled with our things—my family's things—it could go anywhere.

I watched the tent and felt my throat tighten. Blinked hard and rapidly.

And then the tent flew into the branches of a pine tree, just as the wind died down, leaving it trapped up there.

We groaned.

"Who's going to get it?" Mom asked, hands on her hips. It was so high up that we would never be able to reach it with a branch or something.

Ron cracked his knuckles and declared, "I can do it."

We laughed, watching him scramble up the trunk of the pine, the brittle bark peeling under his fingernails and the toes of his Nikes.

"Get down," my mom scolded, hitting his back when he slid all the way down.

He looked at me. "Wait. I can boost you up."

"Pardon?"

Ron raised his eyebrows. "Too scared?"

I grumbled and rolled up my flannel sleeves. "Fine. If you kill me, I'm going to haunt you forever. Like, in a truly horrifying way."

"I can help," my dad offered, squatting in anticipation.

"Yah!" my mom yelled. "Do you want to get another back surgery? Stop that and let the kids do it."

So Ron made a stirrup out of his hands and I stepped onto it, balancing with a wobble. I clutched his shoulder, digging my fingers in a little harder than was necessary. He grunted, but I was able to hoist myself up to one of the larger branches and swing my leg over it so that I was balanced precariously on my butt.

"Be careful!" my mom cried out.

I eyed the tent above me—it was still super high. Heeding my mom's unnecessary warning, I used branches near me to hold my weight as I stood up. Bracing my body against the trunk, I reached up for the tent. But my fingers barely grazed it.

"It's too high!" I shouted down.

"Wait! I have an idea!" my dad said, excited. Too excited. He ran to the car and opened the trunk, unloading a bunch of things before opening the compartment with the spare tire. I squinted as I watched him reach for something. He held it up. A crowbar.

I glanced up, measuring the distance. Might work.

"Okay, toss it up!" I said.

My dad was swinging it back when my mom grabbed it from him. "Wow, are my children and husband intelligent."

She shook her head and went to the car, crowbar in her grasp. After a while, she fished out a nylon rope.

My dad's trunk was like Mary Poppins's carpet bag.

She tied one end around the crowbar, in an expert knot that managed to be both loose and secure.

Ron whistled. "Wow, Mom the Boy Scout."

"Girl Scout. And it's called being practical," she said with a snort. "I don't know how you are both alive, surviving so much stupidity." The words were harsh but said with good humor.

Then she tossed the crowbar-less end of the rope to me... and I caught it. I pulled up the crowbar and untied the rope easily, thanks to my mom's savant rope-tying skills. Something to be discussed at a later date.

I was able to reach the tent with the crowbar and pushed it, hard. It jiggled but didn't dislodge from the branches. I took a breath and tried a couple more times, hearing my family cheer me on below. Well, cheer and heckle. And after the fifth time, it tumbled down, bumping into a few branches before it landed with a gentle thud.

"Yes!" I pumped my fist in the air and my mom applauded loudly. I scrambled back down with Ron's help, and when my feet hit the dirt, I was flushed with victory. When I looked at my family, my irritation with them was gone. Like, not all gone. Because it would always be there. They were my family. It was unavoidable.

But most of it had been swept away from my body like dust in the windstorm. Maybe being lost in the wilderness had reset something within me. In London, I'd tried to break away from the bonds of these people, feeling the whole wide world out there. But I'd always be tied to them. It was just that, now, I knew there would always be some slack—giving me space. And whenever I wanted to, I could pull myself back in. Go back home.

When the tent was packed in a tidy little roll in its nylon case, my dad tossed it into the trunk. "Well, I guess you were right. Time for a new tent."

I stared at it. Suddenly I wanted to curl my body around it, hold it close. Protect it.

"Let's keep it."

My dad looked at me in surprise. "Really?"

I nodded, shutting the trunk with a hard thud. "Let's go home." I wanted to go home, to LA, so badly.

We got into the car and it felt larger. Spacious. And I found myself missing the press of our sleeping bags against each other. The proximity of my family. Always within reach.

ABOUT THE AUTHOR

MAURENE GOO is the author of several critically acclaimed books for young adults, including *I Believe in a Thing Called Love*, *The Way You Make Me Feel*, and *Somewhere Only We Know*.

She lives in Los Angeles with her husband and cat, Maeby.

FIRST WORDS

Varsha Bajaj

My grandparents and parents say America is that shining place across the ocean where scientists make breakthroughs and universities raise brilliant minds. After my brother, Rishi, was born with a hearing impairment, my father created a file of articles that he clipped from newspapers and magazines about sign language, cochlear implants and deaf education in America. "Look," he would say, "look! Progress!" and thrust the article in front of us. The grandparents, aunts and uncles all nodded in awe and agreement. Soon others started bringing Baba articles.

Eight years later, it was a thick file.

Then, one of Baba's colleagues visited New Jersey. He came back with more articles and shining stories about American universities and schools.

The file became even thicker—too thick to ignore.

Baba, a physics researcher, started looking into jobs and visas.

One year later, we're leaving everything we know behind for America and Rishi's future. Everyone thinks we are so lucky. Are we?

The day we got our American visas is carved in my mind like the Om tattooed on Ma's wrist. She gave me a suitcase and said, "Priya, pack carefully. That's all the space you have."

How do you pack your life into a suitcase? I wanted to ask, but I didn't. I knew it was just as hard for Ma and Baba. Ma had packed her spice box and the family idol of Ganesha in her suitcase first. The important things.

Watching me place and remove things from my bag, Ma advised, "Everything has to earn its place." She said, "Take what you truly need and what makes you most happy."

I couldn't pack my collection of smooth rocks, my doll from when I was three or the kite that Baba and I flew every January. I couldn't fit Raj, the boy who made me dream; Aunty Roopa, who lived next door; my best friends; or Dada and Dadi.

I picked my two favorite books, *Little Women* and *Anne of Green Gables*, and wrapped them in the folds of my skirt.

• • •

When we cross through security at the airport, I keep turning back for one more look at my grandparents. Here's where we part ways. I've lived with them all my life, and today I'm leaving them behind. All the elder relatives I know are cared for by their sons. Your children are your security in your old age; it's the Indian way. Dadi and Dada lean on each other for support; selflessly allowing us to secure our future, and for that I want to rush back and hug them one more time.

During the ten-hour flight over the Indian Ocean to London, stray tears roll down my face without permission. Nothing had felt real till the plane abandoned land with a deafening shudder. The roar of the plane seems to say, You've left Bombay, you're going to America. What do you know about it?

We spend hours in Heathrow Airport, dazzled by our first glimpse of the country that ruled us for a gazillion years. We strain to understand the announcements over the speaker system. We worry that they might be important. The words are familiar, but the clipped British accent is difficult to understand. Then we board another plane and cross the Atlantic. Another ocean between us and home. I've lost count of time zones and days.

When we land in New Jersey, I ask Dad, "What day is it?"

"Saturday," he says.

"But it was Saturday when we left Bombay," I say.

"We've traveled back in time," says Dad.

Rishi always signs when we're in loud public places. "Time travelers!"

At the immigration counter the officer stamps the actual, no-time-travel-involved date on my passport: July 23, 1988.

After that twenty-four-hour journey, Dad's cousin drives us to his motel and leads us down a flight of stairs into rooms that are literally under the earth. He calls it the "basement."

It's dark and smells of stale food and liquor, like the train station in Bombay. Rishi runs down the steps two at a time. "Wow!" he says. "Wow!"

Rishi obviously doesn't care about the odors.

Ma and I exchange looks. If we were alone, we would hold our noses.

After his cousin leaves, Baba reminds us, "He's doing us a favor. He's letting us live in his motel, rent free, for as long as we need."

In return Ma and I help their family in every way possible. After school starts in August, I help in the evenings. We clean on our knees and we peel mountains of potatoes. Ma even lets me watch their two-year-old; she says at fifteen, she raised her younger brother.

Dad and Rishi rake mountains of leaves. Those golden leaves, I learn, are dead. I marvel that even death can be beautiful.

Dad reports to his job the Monday after we arrive. Baba has a job teaching physics at a small college. It's how we got a visa to immigrate. Ma, Rishi and I scrub the smell in our rooms away. We wash the little windows that are one foot under the ceiling. Leaves and debris are piled high outside the windows, trapping in gloom. We sweep them away to let the sun shine on the worn, green, holey carpet again.

After buying four airline tickets, there wasn't much money left for anything else. In the new year, we'll have saved enough to move into our own apartment, Baba promises. Some days I ache for my old life, my old friends. I want to be a bird who can fly home across the ocean. When I write to Neena, my best friend in Bombay, I tell her about the apartment we will get soon, and that Dad has bought a car. It was a colleague's old car, but to us it is new. It is our first car.

It takes almost three weeks for my letter to get to Neena. She writes back and asks if we have become rich. In India most people don't have their own cars.

In another letter Neena writes that Raj, the boy I liked in my old school, gave her a tape of Bollywood songs. That day, I scrub the floors extra hard.

Dating might not be allowed, but the heart still beats. My fingers used to tingle when they accidentally touched Raj's as we passed each other test tubes in chem lab back in Bombay. What if I had told Raj that thinking of him made me smile?

It doesn't matter, does it? I am across the world, and Neena is listening to Raj's favorite songs.

Dadi writes a letter telling us she made kheer for my cousins. She isn't one to complain, but we can tell that they'd probably not eaten the kheer with as much joy as Rishi. They had probably not hunted out the raisins and nuts, like I did.

● ● ●

Today Ma's brow is furrowed when I leave for school. Since school started, August, September and October became waves of newness strung into days, and now it's late November.

Like every other day, she reminds me, "Priya, I pray Rishi is okay in school, check on him."

The elementary and high schools are next door to each other.

You're worrying about the wrong kid, I should've told her. He might be hearing impaired and he might have a long way to go with his speech, but he's already found his voice.

It's your "normal" daughter who has been mute in school for more than three months. At first, I knew the exact number of days I hadn't spoken, then I lost count. It's easier to count the few words that I have spoken.

Ma has no way of knowing that; I'd never tell her. It would make the circles under her eyes dark as the night. Ma and Baba say we need to "work hard" to build our new life. I have never slogged so much at school. My hardest class is American History. I have nightmares in which a stern general from the Revolutionary War quizzes me. Last week, the English teacher asked us to diagram a sentence. English has been the language of instruction in my school in Bombay since kindergarten; I have written and read myriad sentences, but never mapped one. My parents know English, but they've never mapped sentences either. Staying after school almost every day for weeks to meet teachers and catch up has become routine. All that learning has left me with no energy to connect with anything but my books.

I watch as Rishi struts into school like it's the only one he's ever known. Maybe it's easier to fit right in if you're eight and in second grade. High school feels like another planet, with different rules and customs, where everyone has attended each other's birthdays since elementary school, except me.

Rishi's smile is his entire face as he signs to his friend, "The bus was tardy!"

He already uses words like *tardy*. We'd never heard that word till we came to New Jersey. Back in Bombay we were just late.

Rishi's voice is louder than it needs to be, and the edges of his words run into each other. He is so busy greeting his friend that he's unaware of the glances that some of the other kids throw his way. With a twinge I realize that I am not the only person who understands him perfectly anymore. When Rishi was little, I was his one and only sister, friend and protector.

As I walk to my school building, a leaf gracefully twirls down and whispers in my ear. I pause and feast on the magnificence of Fall.

I'll write to Dada and Dadi and tell them about this carpet of jeweled red, yellow and gold leaves. Will they believe me? They've never seen anything like it. In Bombay the leaves are always green. They don't transform and remind us that everything changes. If only I had a camera.

Baba reads a lot of science fiction. One day, he says, we'll all have phones with cameras. I'll be like old and forty by then.

● ● ●

They were right though, all the aunts and uncles and grandparents and parents. Rishi's speech has already improved with the new hearing aids he got last month. We could never have bought hearing aids of that quality in Bombay. His residual hearing has also improved. His school has a deaf education classroom where he learns for part of the day, and it has made all the difference.

When Ma and Baba were told the class was free and part of the public-school services, Ma cried. Then she lit incense and the oil lamp to thank God for making it all possible.

"He will not be held back in America." I hear their chorus as I walk into my classroom and take my seat.

At roll call I raise my hand but don't say, "Here," like the others.

I said four words on the first day of school. When my eraser fell to the floor and rolled slowly under my classmate Jane's desk, I pointed and said, "My rubber."

Jane's eyes opened wide. "What?" she said.

"My rubber," I repeated.

Jane's face turned red. The kids around us were laughing.

A giant boy who sat across the aisle fished in his pocket and waved a packet at me. "I got one too, baby."

I knew what it was. To control the exploding population rates, India ran advertisements on TV and billboards encouraging the use of condoms.

"Shut up, Brett!" I heard Jane say. She picked up what I soon learned to call my eraser and handed it back to me. Her eyes connected with mine and seemed to say, Don't worry about him and the others, they don't understand. Or that is what I told myself.

My eyes might have been moist, so I lowered them but not before noticing Jane's barely perceptible nod that said, You're okay.

That day, my words shriveled up, but Jane's kindness stayed with me, like a shawl wrapped around my shoulders on a cold day.

A little voice in my head said, If you don't speak, they can't laugh at you, but they won't know you either.

The quieter I became, the more I could hear. My classmates might not know me, but I got to know them and their whispered secrets. Megan told her friends that she had taken glamor shots at the mall and wanted to be a model. I sideglanced and saw the pictures; she looked like a movie star. Jane moved to this school last year. She has lived in five countries,

and her father's job requires them to move a lot. She knows
how it feels to be the new kid.

• • •

I am becoming comfortable in my silent cocoon. Everyone is busy in their own worlds; there are standardized tests,
extracurricular activities, kids thinking about college. Most
girls who smiled at me at first have stopped trying. My English teacher required an oral recitation of a poem, but she
also offered the option of writing an essay. I was the only one
who chose the essay, even though it involved more work.

When I get off the bus at the end of the day, I clear my
throat in the cold windy air. My brother gets off his bus at the
same time. He starts to excitedly tell me about his day using a
combination of words and signs. I laugh. My unused tongue
reshapes words again. I can still speak to him.

As we run down the steps to our basement rooms, we
smell cardamoms, sugar, tea and milk, boiling and steeping
into the perfect chai.

Once inside, I place my backpack next to the shelves built
with cement blocks and planks of wood where I have ar-
ranged my books.

Little Women and *Anne of Green Gables*. The two classic
books that I first read aloud with Dada and Dadi. They gave
me these books almost five years ago, on my tenth birthday.

The books sit by their picture. They wait for our weekly
phone call. Calls are expensive, more than two dollars a minute, and make me miss them more. I cannot touch or smell or
feel their arms around me over the static-filled phone lines.

But I can remember reading aloud with Dada, as he sat in his favorite rocking chair, his voice lilting and excited.

"I have never seen snow," he said when we read about the March girls walking through the snow on Christmas Day. One day, I hope that he and Dadi will visit, and we'll walk through snow together.

When Dada and I read *Anne of Green Gables*, we agreed that Marilla, with her quiet, no-nonsense strength, was just like Dadi, who was listening even as her fingers expertly knotted jasmine flowers into a garland. These books still feel warm from the touch of my grandparents' hands.

"Priya." Ma calls for me to join them.

Rishi slurps his tea. "I made a new friend today," he announces.

Ma's smile lights up her face. "If you're both happy, this is all worth it."

I make up a story about having a friend too, because that smile on Ma's face is a reward.

"Ma, Jane said she liked my shirt. I told her about how you and I picked the cloth from the fabric store near our house in Bombay and how you sewed it for me," I lie.

Jane did speak to me; she pointed to my top and said, "It's so pretty."

I should've responded. I want to talk with Jane. Yet I didn't say a word to her.

A nod and a smile were all I could manage.

My English doesn't sound like Jane's. What if she doesn't understand me? What if I make a fool of myself again?

Everything is so foreign, like the trees that drop gold leaves, the kids in high school who drive cars, the lockers in which we're supposed to store books, and the couples who kiss and embrace openly in the cafeteria. I had never seen two people kiss on the lips before in real life, only in Hollywood films, and I almost choked on my food. In Bollywood films, the actors don't kiss on the lips. The camera discreetly moves away during intimate moments.

That evening, I take a break from homework and helping Mom and watch *Full House* on the TV in the motel communal living room. I listen carefully to how the actors roll their *R*s and slant their *A*s. One day I imagine having hair like DJ's. I want jeans that hug my hips like DJ's do, and a shirt that I can tuck into the waistband. My shirts hang around my hips.

• • •

I am sitting on a bench by a mural of books, open, flying, on shelves and suspended in space, in the most magical room I've ever known, when the school librarian says, "Listen up. I'm starting a book club. It's open to everyone." She holds a book high with both hands and does a dance. "This is our first selection. We're starting with the classics."

The room spins.

Little Women.

Her copy is exactly like mine, with the same logo of a penguin in its orange egg on the cover.

I don't hear anything after that, because the Atlantic Ocean separating me from my grandparents roars in my ears.

I blame the heady smell of the books, and the sound of those waves, for the words that almost escape my mouth.

Right before they take flight, though, I reel them back like a kite on a string.

Without realizing it, I have risen to my feet in excitement, my mouth open. Everyone notices.

Kids giggle.

I look around and slump back into my seat.

But for a nanosecond, my eyes lock with Mrs. Kennedy's. She smiles.

"I have a sign-up sheet on my desk," she says.

As I pass her on my way out, the librarian places her hand on my shoulder. "We'll chat about the girls and Marmee while we eat lunch. I hope you come."

I can't imagine anything more wonderful.

Speak, my brain commands.

I don't listen. I nod.

I have so much I want to tell Mrs. Kennedy. I'd tell her that, once I start speaking, I won't stop. My best friends in Bombay always said I talked too much. I'd tell her that I have never seen a library as beautiful as hers. Could she recommend a book for me to read?

Somehow, I know that she will understand.

All the words imprisoned throughout the day escape on the bus ride to the grocery store that evening. I tell Ma and Rishi about the book club.

"Will your friend Jane be there?" Ma asks.

I blink. One of these days my lies will catch up with me. I don't know if she'll be there, but I want Ma to think Jane is my friend. I lie again. "Yes, yes she will."

Excited, Rishi says, "You have to go. That's your favorite book."

In the grocery store Rishi points to a jar of peanut butter.

"What's that?" Ma asks.

"It's what all the kids eat," Rishi signs. "Priya can make a peanut butter sandwich for her book club. It's during lunch."

I know what she'll say next. "Is it expensive?"

"We have to stop converting everything into rupees," I say.

Ma checks the price and puts the jar in our cart.

On the bus ride home, Rishi signs and again asks, "When is the book club?"

I sign back and tell Rishi I'm not going.

He looks at me surprised. "Why?" he signs.

"I don't know anyone," I say.

He raises his eyebrows and challenges me.

"Of course, you do," he signs. "You know the girls from the book."

His words sink in and call me out.

Wait.

When did he get so smart? I do know the March girls, and although they are characters in a book, they are real to me.

I hold on to his hand. This little brother of mine has grown up and become so wise in a few short months. Rishi has thrived despite his obstacles. He is a survivor and is inspiring me to be the same. I might have taken care of him when we were little, but today, he is showing me the way. It might not have been my choice to come to America, but I am here. I must keep marching.

●●●

On Tuesday, I wake early. My hair lies flat on my head. How do all the girls in school have high and curly hair, with a poofy roll up front, that adds at least an inch to their height? I try to get my hair to poof up, but it won't. I have seen a girl spray her hair in the bathroom. Maybe that's what does it. I don't have magic in a can.

Rishi does notice that it looks different and points and signs, "What's wrong with your hair?"

Oh no! I run to the bathroom to try and flatten it back down, because Rishi is right. It looks like a nest of hay.

Rishi helps me cut the crusts off the bread and open the jar of peanut butter. We all smell it and take a taste.

"It tastes like besan ladoos," says Ma.

She is right; it tastes like the chickpea flour sweets from home.

All morning, my heart races. Is Jane going to book club? She was there when the librarian announced it three weeks ago, but I didn't see her sign up, so probably not. I could ask her, but that would mean speaking words aloud.

Then the last class before lunch, social studies, is done. It is still my hardest class.

I see a group of girls heading toward the library, laughing, their arms linked. I stop in my friendless tracks.

What am I doing? I don't belong.

I don't know anyone.

They carry their lunches in brown paper bags. I might have a peanut butter sandwich instead of the chutney and cucumber one that Ma typically makes, but it's still not right. Mine is wrapped in a plastic grocery bag. My clothes are not stylish either, they were made by my mother. They don't look like anyone else's.

I remember Jo from *Little Women* going to New York, alone, in her unstylish clothes. She did not let the big city defeat her.

They all had their shirts tucked in. I can do that. I slip into the bathroom and tuck my loose shirt into my pants. In the mirror, I look different. My hips are outlined like the other girls'. I smile at my reflection. One day I might have a friend, and maybe she'll help me with my hair. I might even own hairspray.

I square my shoulders, clutch my copy of *Little Women* and my lunch and race to the library. Yes, I might make a mistake again, but I will live, and I will learn.

I turn the knob on the door. It is closed. It's not usually locked, but maybe Mrs. Kennedy doesn't want interruptions. I am late.

Defeated, I walk away.

Then I hear Mrs. Kennedy's voice, calling me. I turn around. She stands there with the door wide open and smiles. "Priya! Come in. I'm so happy you decided to join us."

The kids are sitting by the castle. Jane is there too. It is a complete closed circle.

They are busy eating, chatting. Nobody notices me.

I stand outside the group.

Mrs. Kennedy clears her throat, "Everyone, let's make the circle bigger and make room for one more. Priya, get a chair."

Chairs scrape on the floor and the circle widens.

Jane has jumped up and brought me a chair.

As she places my chair in the group, she whispers, "I hoped you'd come."

This time, I squeeze her hand, and my eyes promise friendship.

Then Mrs. Kennedy says, "Let's start the discussion by sharing who your favorite character is, and why."

I take a deep breath. I must do this.

"Jo March," I say loudly and clearly.

My fifth and sixth words float into the air like a kite, and this time I don't reel them back.

ABOUT THE AUTHOR

VARSHA BAJAJ is the award-winning author of picture books and middle grade novels. Her middle grade novels are *Count Me In* and *Abby Spencer Goes to Bollywood*, which was shortlisted for the Cybils Award and included in the Spirit of Texas Reading program. Her picture books include *The Home Builders*, and *This is Our Baby, Born Today*, a Bank Street Best Book. She grew up in Mumbai, India, and when she came to the United States to obtain her master's degree, her adjustment to the country was aided by her awareness of the culture through books.

• • •

FAMILY
EVERYTHING
Yamile Saied Méndez

• • •

To Florencia, Mauricio, and Gabriel, my dear friends
who became my family when I was alone in a strange country,
trying to learn a new language and find out who I really was.
And to my family who's always with me in spite of the time
and distance we're physically apart. ¡Los quiero!

Ayelén hated translating on the spot. It was one thing to transcribe the lyrics of the last Backstreet Boys songs for her friends or the recipe of upside-down pineapple cake for her mom. Translating her good news in front of the family and even some friends who'd seen her grow up was quite another. The expectation, in some cases tinged with doubt, of the people in the room had given Ayelén the wings to try the impossible, and now it was time to confirm that all her work had paid off.

The fact that they all knew what she was about to say didn't make things easier. As soon as Ayelén had received the letter the night before, her parents had marched to the locutorio and called everyone. Their phone had been out of service for months for lack of payment. Every cent had been saved for her education.

Now that everyone wanted to hear the news from her mouth, the doubts came from her own heart and pulled her down like an anchor. She felt she was in one of those flying dreams gone wrong.

The thick paper shook in her hands. For the first time, she noticed it had been postmarked three weeks ago. Even in the year 2000, life-changing news—history-making news—took its sweet time to arrive in her small town of San Lorenzo, beyond the city of Rosario in Argentina.

"Read," her father nudged her softly, luminous pride in his voice.

She locked her knees so that her legs wouldn't tremble. The trick worked, but only until she realized her padrino's stare was trained on the paper as if the letter would sprout teeth and fangs and ravage her hands.

Padrino's house held its breath to catch every word. The only sounds were the fútbol commentary from the neighbor's radio, the shifting of her little cousins' sandaled feet, and the hum of the blue-bellied refrigerator.

"Read," Nadia and Selena, her little cousins, urged. Santino, the baby, cried, and Daiana, the only cousin her age, hurried toward her bedroom, to feed him most likely.

In her mind, Ayelén read in English and the words transformed into Spanish. When nerves got the better of her and the rising emotion clouded her sight, the words on the paper swam like the noodles in the soup Abuela used to make when she was still alive. But Ayelén remembered every word, comma, and period. She'd read it hundreds of times, afraid that the words would change, that she had misinterpreted their meaning, or worse, that she'd imagined it all.

"Ayelén Sofía Abad…" The words sounded like a blessing. "You have been accepted to Brigham Young University for our Spring semester starting on April 29th…"

Applause and cheers erupted before she could finish the first sentence. Even the little cousins who didn't know what the words meant celebrated the victory, which had been generations in the making. Even Malón, the aging husky, barked like he did whenever Rosario Central, the family's favorite soccer team, scored a goal. All her life, Ayelén knew that family was above everything, and that a victory for one was a victory for all.

After hugs and kisses, Madrina María Laura clapped and the women got busy frying empanadas, making the chimichurri, and setting the table, while Helena, Ayelén's mom, boasted about her daughter. The men drifted toward the parrilla, the bricked-walled grill, where the fire had been waiting for el asado. Ayelén hesitated, unsure if her place was with the women making the meal or the men discussing politics and fútbol while they drank máte and beer.

On the back patio, her cousins jumped rope. They chanted the same song Ayelén and Daiana had sung on the patio years and years ago. At seventeen, she still knew all the words.

"Arroz con leche, me quiero casar…"

In the past, before she got her letter, before Daiana had her baby, her cousin had been Ayelén's refuge, her companion on adventures and in dreaming. She was the only one who understood the weight of so many expectations. Now Ayelén was alone, severed from her people, far from them already.

Throughout the afternoon, she read the letter time after time to anyone who asked her to, and she tried to explain where the university was (nestled in the mountains in the Western United States, where the church her family went to was established), and who she was going to live with (she had no idea). The only one who didn't ask for more details was her padrino, Tío Alí. He gazed at her with such sadness that Ayelén had the urge to turn back time to the night before, when she was still a girl dreaming and not the chosen one expected to save them all.

In January, the sun went down late, and after another meal of homemade pizzas and leftover asado, as the frogs sang their nightly song and the bats circled the sky under the silver moon, visitors trickled back to their homes and lives. Soon the only ones left were Ayelén, her parents, and her brothers, Lautaro and Francisco. They slept on the couch protected by the mosquito repellent coil's smoke while the little cousins tried to catch lightning bugs and crickets.

Madrina María Laura called them in and ushered them to bed. It was time to go, and Daiana had never left the room she now shared with her baby.

"We better go," Ayelén's dad said, just when she'd gathered the courage to walk toward her cousin's closed door. "We have to work tomorrow. There's so much to do before April."

In the US, school usually started in September, but her English teacher had encouraged her to apply for Spring term, when there were fewer incoming students. Ayelén was grateful she'd followed the advice, but April was just around the corner.

Madrina helped Ayelén's mom herd the boys into their old car, a Renault 12 held together by prayers and miracles.

"Felicidades, Farid. You won," Padrino said, as if he'd hoped to end with the last word.

She winced at the bitterness lacing Padrino's voice, and worse, his words. Her dad had won?

After a few seconds of charged silence, Padrino added, "You proved she could do it, but sending her by herself is too dangerous. You can't let her go."

The unspoken words were, If you let her go and anything bad happens to her, it will be your fault. If you let her go, it will mean you're a bad father.

Ayelén had never meant to leave on her own. The family's shared dream had been for her and Daiana to go together.

Ayelén looked at her father, afraid that all her work had been for nothing. It wouldn't be the first time her father's mind had changed after a word from his brother.

Ayelén had literally burned her eyelashes in candlelight to keep studying when the power went off in their cinderblock apartment, located in a neighborhood of government housing. Her mom cleaned houses after she came home from cashiering at the supermarket. Her little brothers made do with hand-me-downs and no birthday parties. And her dad spent backbreaking hours in a taxi, risking his life during the hours when taxi drivers were most vulnerable to the rampant crime in the city, to earn another one-hundred-peso note that could salvage the night.

A teacher, Mrs. Orán, had told Ayelén that such dedication was commendable, but had she considered the need for moderation?

The teacher didn't understand, but Padrino did. Now he wanted to take all that away because his ego was wounded.

Her father glanced at Ayelén, and as if they'd rehearsed the next step, she grabbed her father's hand.

Padrino's face hardened. The spark of struggle in his eyes intensified.

"Farid, think about it," he pleaded. "Our abuelo Amir arrived in this country with a hand in front and another behind. He didn't speak a word of Spanish, and he built this house with his own hands. Did he do all that for nothing? For your daughter to run away when things get hard here? The country needs all of us. La patria se hace trabajando. And the United States isn't a place to send a girl like her alone. Believe me. I watch the movies and the news, Farid. In the United States, everyone is on their own."

Her father's voice was strong when he said, "Ayelén will never be on her own. She will always have us. At least she will have Helena, the boys, and me." He looked at Ayelén. "Let's go, hija."

The little cousins, Nadia and Selena, stood quiet by the door, their eyes like wet river stones, shiny and dark. Ayelén knelt to hug them, hoping this wouldn't be the last time.

• • •

In the months that followed, Ayelén and the whole family threw themselves into preparations for her trip. Her ancestors, Abuelo Amir and Abuela Elizabeta, and all the others whose names had been lost, had crossed the oceans in ships for which they sometimes had a ticket but most times did not. She'd fly in an airplane, with the cheapest ticket they could find, the one that stopped in every country in Latin America, slowly inching its way north.

"Keep la yerba in the original package at all times in case the police think it's something else," Helena reminded Ayelén when they were repacking her backpack the night before the trip.

Ayelén nodded and wrapped the yerba package in the plastic wrap her family had never dared splurge on before. Unlike her ancestors, who'd arrived with only the clothes on their backs, Ayelén had a small suitcase and a backpack into which she stuffed as many of her belongings as possible. But although she asked her departed abuelos for instructions, they wouldn't tell her how to pack the memory of jasmín del Paraguay and fireworks exploding on Noche Buena, or the taste of Helena's canelones with red sauce that she made on special occasions like farewells. She didn't know how to bottle the scent of Lautaro's hair after playing fútbol in the rain. Or the touch of Francisco's tiny five-year-old hand on her face.

"And remember to put your documents in the leather pouch," Farid said.

The leather pouch had been a gift from Lucrecia at Transatlantic Travel. The travel agent had smiled first in surprise and then in admiration and at the end in plain congratulations when Ayelén had shown up every month with a white envelope hidden inside her math book to pay the plane fare, bit by bit.

All night long, a parade of family and friends, close, distant and twice removed, came to leave good wishes, all they could afford, to the first girl in three generations to leave the tree and branch out on her own. Although no one said it at the time, they left with the seed of wonder and possibility. That night, boys and girls all over the city dreamed that maybe they too could do impossible things. Mothers and fathers lay in bed, eyes wide open, thinking upon their lives and the dreams they'd forgotten in the day-to-day struggle of making things work, of rebuilding the country when it kept falling apart time after time.

Ayelén lay in bed too, waiting for a call from her padrino to send her off with his blessing. But although they'd finally paid the overdue bill, the phone stayed silent.

In the morning, the benteveos sang before the sun came up and burned the fog; fall was creeping in just in time for Easter. Ayelén got up to share the last mátes with her parents before the boys woke up. They drank the tea with sugar. Life already had too much bitterness. There wasn't time for more last-minute advice.

Ayelén worried that she was betraying her family and country for having the outlandish dream of testing her boundaries and seeing how far she could go, but she had to be stronger than her doubts and unfurl her wings.

"Remember who you are," her father said.

The truth was that she wasn't sure who she really was. Wasn't that why she was leaving? To find out?

When Helena wasn't looking, the boys gifted their sister their favorite Ferrari Hot Wheels, the ones they'd gotten for Christmas like three years ago that still looked brand new. Her brothers watched with wonder as she headed downstairs, followed by a train of neighbors, who waved goodbye.

At the Rosario international airport, the family closed their eyes and huddled for a whispered prayer that Helena offered with contained emotion. She was trying so hard to remain strong. When Ayelén opened her eyes, she saw her cousin

Daiana running in her direction, her black hair whipping behind her. Ayelén hugged the sister of her heart for the first time since Santino's baptism. In the look they shared, they tried to tell each other that the years of competition had been the most fun they'd ever had. That although the journey was taking them in seemingly opposite directions, they were both moving forward. They were both so young.

"Send me pictures and call me when you arrive," Daiana said, pressing a piece of paper into Ayelén's hand. "I know it's expensive, but my friend Florencia said there are calling cards. She'll be there when you arrive—"

A speaker announced Ayelén's flight, but Ayelén nodded so that her cousin would know she was grateful beyond words for Daiana connecting her to a friend who was studying in Utah, even though their fathers hadn't been talking.

Her family gathered around her like chicks before the first gust of a storm, but Ayelén was ready to fly.

Her mother composed herself first and gently pushed her toward the escalator.

"Chau, chau!" little voices cried.

"Te queremos!"

"Make us proud!"

And last, "Don't forget us!"

Her mother had told her not to look back. And so, like the maligned woman of the Bible story she'd studied in Sunday school, Ayelén fought the temptation to take one last look.

Before she stepped on the escalator, she lost the fight and turned around.

Love blazed in the faces of her loved ones.

Ayelén didn't turn into a salt statue, but salt rose in her

throat, and although she'd never seen the sea in her life, some part of her DNA remembered that tears tasted like sea water, the same sea that had brought her family to this land. This land she was now leaving.

Beyond the little huddle, Padrino looked at her with tears in his eyes. Ayelén waved him over. He hesitated for a second, and then as if he were wading through cement, he made his way to her. So did her father.

Ayelén took Padrino's hand and her father's. "It was never a competition. Remember, a victory for one is a victory for all."

Both men lowered their heads, chastised. The weight they'd put on her shoulders was too hard for a kid to carry. When they let go of her hands, Padrino said, "You earned it all. Now go and be happy. We'll be cheering for you."

● ● ●

Once, Ayelén had asked her mother how she'd learned how to be a mother, how she'd learned what the twins' cries meant and how to soothe them. Her mother had laughed and confessed she'd been pretending since day one.

"Fake it till you make it," she'd said and continued making perfect gnocchi balls for Sunday dinner.

Fake it till you make it—that's what Ayelén tried to do.

She faked confidence until she reached customs somewhere in Texas.

When the immigration officer asked her where she was going, she tightened her fist around her talisman: Daiana's note with little drawings from Nadia and Selena, hearts that united a stick figure labeled Ayelén to a giant heart labeled Your familia.

In a clear voice, she replied, "I'm starting college next week."

Maybe the brown-skinned, young immigration officer saw all the dreams flashing in Ayelén's eyes. Without more questions, he stamped her passport and smiled. "Come on in," he said. "Welcome to the United States."

She could manage only to mumble her gratitude. She was in a daze.

When her final flight arrived in Salt Lake City and there was no sign of her ride, she pretended a primal fear wasn't clawing at her chest. She pushed it down, until she calmed herself enough to buy a calling card so that she could dial the phone number Daiana had given her so long ago, when they'd both been young girls sunbathing on a rooftop without a care in the world.

"Hola?" said a young girl's voice, and her heart leaped. Ayelén hadn't been away for more than fourteen hours, and she already missed the sound of her language on her people's tongues.

"Florencia?" Ayelén asked. "It's me, Ayelén, at the airport."

A pair of little boys were playing by the telephone, and she had to look away from them, pretending she didn't miss her little brothers with an intensity that made her weak.

"I'm almost there," Florencia said. "I'll meet you at baggage claim!"

Ten minutes later, Ayelén was laughing with Florencia, a girl she'd never met before, but who, after a tight hug, already felt like a friend.

With Florencia, there were two boys, Argentine transplants too. One was tall and dark haired and talked nonstop—Mauricio. The other, Gabriel, smiled shyly. In the car to Provo, where the school was located, Ayelén realized he wasn't really shy. Although he'd been born in Buenos Aires, he didn't speak that much Spanish.

The kids in the car pointed at every landmark, translating on the spot, filling her in on all the info she'd need to start out. She hardly knew more than their names and the fútbol teams they supported, but inside her, the voice of her ancestors told her this was a good start.

The Wasatch Mountains, still covered in their white winter coats, towered along the highway. She tried to memorize everything so that when she called her family, she could tell them every detail. In a way, they would be with her, seeing through her eyes.

She had her family supporting her from afar, an anchor and wings, all at the same time.

ABOUT THE AUTHOR

YAMILE (sha-MEE-lay) **SAIED MÉNDEZ** is a fútbol-obsessed Argentine American author who loves meteor showers, summer, astrology, and pizza. She lives in Utah with her Puerto Rican husband and their five kids, two adorable dogs, and one majestic cat. An inaugural Walter Dean Myers Grant and a New Visions Award Honor recipient, she's also a graduate of Voices of Our Nations (VONA) and the Vermont College of Fine Arts MFA in Writing for Children and Young Adults program. She's a founding member of Las Musas, a marketing collective of women and nonbinary Latinx children's authors. Find her online at yamilesmendez.com.

• • •

WHEN I WAS WHITE

Justine Larbalestier

• • •

For Mikki Kendall

Never knew I was white til I met Joshua.

I was sixteen and knew nuthin.

"My money's as good as anyone else's, miss," he said.

My mind was elsewhere, gazing out the shop front, past the onions on strings, the tinned pears, the rack of magazines, imagining meself dancing like Irene Castle, skirts flaring around me like wings, and Vernon's hands on me waist, swirling me round and round, and everyone clapping.

"Miss, I'm leaving this money on the counter and taking the gum. Damn it. I need change. I'm pretty sure I'm giving you too much. Look—I don't want trouble, I want to pay with your nonsensical money—what is a farthing?—and go, miss?"

He snapped his fingers.

I blinked. Daydream scattered.

"Sorry?" I stared at the handsome brown-skinned foreigner in front of me. Me cheeks went hot. His eyes were dreamy.

"Thank you, miss," he said. His smile made his eyes dreamier. "I've always thought so too."

"Thought what?"

"That my eyes are dreamy."

I never said that out loud, did I?

I bloody did.

"What's your name, miss?" he asked, leaning over the counter. His teeth was white and not a one missing.

"Dulcie."

"Dulcie. Pretty name."

It were when he said it.

"Tosh. It's dead common."

Like me. I'd always wanted a fancy name like Violet or Esmeralda.

"You're not common, sugar. With those big green eyes."

I laughed at his fib.

There weren't enough water to wash that morning. The dress I was wearing used to be my aunt's, and her boss's before her, and the only reason I'd eaten was cause old Mister Wong hadn't caught me swiping cheese and bread yet.

I was common as.

He wasn't. He smelled like peppermint, his hat sat at an angle and weren't shiny from age.

"How old are you?"

"Twenty," I lied. "You?"

"Twenty-two," he said. "Not many customers."

He picked up the gum, turned it around, set it down. His fingernails were neat, with no dirt under them.

"They're at work, if they've got it, and if they don't, they're out looking or still asleep."

"What kind of work?"

"Making clothes or at the brewery. No one'll be in here for hours."

"Fortunate for us."

Fortunate. He was dead posh.

"You talk funny," I said. "Like the movies. Whatcha doing here?"

He leaned forward to whisper, "I'm lost."

I giggled.

He saluted. "Joshua P. Desmond Irving the Third. At your service."

"The Third? You an African king, then?"

"If I am, will you kiss me?"

Me face got hot and other bits of me too. "I'll kiss ya either way," I said, and I did.

He tasted like vanilla and laughter. He made me heart beat so fast I was woozy.

● ● ●

When we walked down the street together I was dead proud. Joshua was handsomer than any of the Hills fellas.

I didn't mind Tiny Bruce yelling at us.

Johnno O'Rourke.

Tommy Newton too.

Calling us a bunch of names I'd never heard.

They said it weren't natural, us being together. Me Irish, him dark.

But I reckon they was jealous.

Joshua tightened his hand on mine and muttered about this godforsaken city in this godforsaken country.

He didn't like the Hills. He didn't like Sydney. He didn't like Australia.

I reckoned they was all right but I'd never been nowhere else.

• • •

Three weeks after he startled me out of me daydream, he pulled me into a new one: Joshua asked me to scarper with him.

"Too right, I will."

I kissed Ma goodbye. I thought she was gunna be filthy but all she said was, "Send us some jingle soon as youse get some."

I weren't gunna miss her neither. She weren't much of a mum and we was skint. Four of us in one room: Ma, her latest fella, the new baby, me, and only me with steady work.

Her new fella was handsy. Wouldn't miss him a bit.

I'd've gone anywhere with anyone. But someone as dreamy as Joshua? That were a bloody miracle.

He told me not to bring any clothes. He'd sort it.

• • •

On the boat he told me about his home, Harlem.

I'd never heard of it.

He told me about his people promenading along the avenue—Seventh Avenue, that is—in their Sunday best, wearing furs, hats, gloves, strutting and striving.

"Furs?" I asked, though I wanted to know what strutting and striving was. "Like in the movies?"

"Like in the movies."

Everyone danced to jazz in nightclubs.

People in the Hills danced to jigs on sawdust-floored pubs, then, after six o'clock closing, out on the street.

"Is jazz like a jig?"

"A little bit," he said, but I could tell it wasn't. Joshua was laughing at me. I didn't mind. He could do anything he liked long as he didn't send me back to the Hills.

"They won't mind me not being dark like you?"

"You'll be black."

I stared. I was an Irish bluey: red hair, green eyes, porridge-pale, freckle-coated skin.

"No one's gunna believe I'm black. Look at me freckles!"

"My freckles." He pointed at his nose and cheeks. "What are these?"

"They ain't freckles like mine."

"Don't say ain't."

What else were I supposed to say?

"Sorry, Dulcie," he said, kissing my cheek. "Habit. Bad habit. It's just, well, if you don't want to seem common, you shouldn't talk common."

I was common.

Irish too. I couldn't decide to be a whole different Dulcie cause Joshua said so. Though I'd give it me best if it'd keep him from chucking me.

"Don't worry," he said. "Being white is a state of mind."

"Huh? White? I'm Irish. Me ma's people are from county Cork."

Joshua laughed. "Black Irish. People see what they want to: curly hair and sugar lips. There's your one drop."

One drop of what?

• • •

Joshua gave me a ring on the boat. He had a matching one
for himself.

"We're married now." He kissed me. "Hello, Mrs. Dulcie Irving."

I knew we wasn't. You need a proper ceremony and government papers for that.

"That mean I'm Mrs. Dulcie Irving the Third now?"

He laughed so hard his hat fell off.

• • •

On the boat, we washed daily. Sometimes more. Heaven.

He taught me to dance fancy. Like the Castles. The dresses
he bought me flared.

"This is fun," I shouted as we twirled.

"It is, isn't?" He was beaming. I could see my smile reflected in his eyes.

• • •

We was on that boat forever.

He give me loads of books, explaining the words I didn't
know: *capitalism, audacious, angst, juxtaposition, algebra, discom-
bobulated.*

He told me how they come from the Latin! German!
French! Arabic!

"Pyjamas was originally a Persian word. Or possibly Urdu.
Isn't that extraordinary?"

"Yes," I breathed, kissing him, tasting his enthusiasm.

I'd never heard any of those languages, saving German.
The Schwartzes on Devonshire talked Kraut.

Joshua had to show me on a map where all those places

were, where America was and Australia too, and the giant ocean in between, holding the boat afloat.

Africa, Joshua said, pointing to it, was where black people come from. Europe was white people's homeland. Joshua pointed to Ireland in Europe. It was tiny. Being from Ireland meant I was also from Europe, which made me white. Except that when we got to Harlem, he wanted me to be black.

I'd never been white or black before. I wanted to stay Irish.

While I tried to read, stumbling over every third word, Joshua wrote. He had a typing machine that was loud as thunder.

The noise did me head in, so I'd go out on the deck with one of his books, read a few pages. Soon I'd be watching the waves, and the book would be in me lap.

Saw a whale that way. Its tail sticking up glossy from the water.

"A whale," he said when I told him, smiling at this impossible thing. "Did you know that word's from the Old English?"

There were parts of the boat we couldn't go. That bothered Joshua. I didn't care. Where we could go was plenty.

I didn't need anything else.

Or anyone else.

Joshua was the smartest, handsomest, funniest man I ever met. I tried to talk, smile and laugh like him.

But it was sand copying water.

NEW YORK CITY, 1932

Harlem was everything Joshua said. All the punters was dressed beautiful. New gloves, hats and the shiniest shoes. So many rich people.

And they were mostly black. I'd never seen so many.

"Stop staring," Joshua said.

There's hearing, then there's seeing.

"Well, she's like me," I said, nodding at a girl with blonde curls in a navy blue suit with matching hat, shoes and bag. There was a giant blue bow in her hair.

She wasn't, though. She was fancy and walked like a dancer.

"No, she's black too. I told you, it's one drop here."

"Everyone's black? Even the ones who look Irish?"

"Mostly. Stop staring."

• • •

And Joshua's home?

A bloody mansion. Three stories high! He had his own floor!

Joshua didn't tell me he was a writer. A writer! I knew he wrote—he had that machine—but who knew that could be your job?

Joshua didn't tell me his daddy ran a funeral parlour and had investments—no one told me what those were—and his mother wore fur coats. Not one—many—and the best one mink!

His sister was a lawyer, his oldest brother a doctor and the middle one a mechanic.

My sister was dead and me brother out bush and then there was the baby.

I knew he was fancy: the way he talked, the way he dressed, but on the boat we was—we were—we been—in the lower decks, not up top with the snobs.

I'd figured he was down on his luck.

He was not.

He was never gunna keep me.

• • •

I'll never forget walking in, everything gleaming but the carpets. The wood shone. The walls. The lights hanging from the ceiling.

I was unsteady from the boat, and terrified from the fancy.

An old woman with curly white hair and darker skin than Joshua, in a pretty grey dress, opened the door.

"Josh, baby," she said, pulling him into her arms, then pushing him back. "Handsome as ever. Who's this?" she said, turning to me.

The smile on her face slipped.

"This is my wife."

"Your wife!" she said. "Well, well…" She trailed off, stuck on that one word. "Well, isn't she sweet?" she said at last, patting my shoulder.

I shook her hand. "I'm Dulcie. Nice to meet ya, Mrs Irving."

She laughed. "Oh no. I'm not Mrs Irving. I'm Eula. I look after—"

"I'm Mrs Irving," a beautiful lady on the stairs said. Her steps were silent on the carpet.

She was wearing a fur coat. Jewels glittered in her ears, her hair, around her neck.

Oh no. Why couldn't Eula be his mum?

"Your wife?" she asked. It sounded like she was asking if I was his dog. "Is that legal?"

"It's legal here, Mama, in New York State."

Joshua squeezed my hand.

"You'd best not travel."

"This is my wife, Mama, Dulcie Irving."

"Hello, Mrs Irving." I dropped Joshua's hand to do a curtsy, like I'd seen on the news reels. Joshua steadied me.

Mrs Irving looked me over like I was something bad stuck on her shoe.

I put out my hand—clean, even under the nails—I'd washed that morning. She took it in her gloved one, then dropped it fast.

I bit my tongue to stop meself from telling her I didn't have no diseases.

She turned her cheek to Joshua. He kissed the air next to it.

"Mama," he said.

"You look well, Joshua. We'll eat in, Eula. Two extras for dinner. Cold cuts will do."

"Will Otis and Jesse join us?" Joshua asked.

Mrs Irving handed her gloves to Eula.

"I asked if Otis will join us?"

"I heard you."

Eula took her coat. She wore a shiny, tight dress underneath, like a movie star.

"Gorgeous dress, Mrs Irving."

She winced.

"What did she say, Joshua, darling?" she asked as if I weren't talking English same as her.

"She admired your dress."

As she glided down the hall I thought I heard her whisper to herself.

I wanted to yell after her that I'm Irish trash, thank you very much.

• • •

The next night Joshua took me to a salon. It was people sitting in chairs in someone's house, smoking, drinking, reading out loud, and arguing.

Everyone was older, smarter, fancier than me.

A smiling dark-skinned woman with a wide mouth and freckles on her cheekbones told me her name was Zee. She asked me what kind of writer I was. She was wearing a blue hat and a necklace of red beads.

"No kind," I mumbled. I can hardly read. "I'm Joshua's missus."

"His wife? Well," Zee said, like Eula had, only she didn't get stuck on it. She turned to Joshua, "Married!" She punched him gently on the arm. "To Miss Anne!"

"My name is Dulcie," I said. They didn't hear.

"She's not, Zee." He smiled at me. "She's Australian. Irish. Black Irish."

"Well, isn't she a long way from home? Your saditty mama must love her."

"She hates me," I said. I wondered what saditty meant. I said it a few times, quiet-like, so I could remember to look it up later. Joshua had shown me how.

"As you'd expect," Joshua said. They laughed.

I was about to sit next to Joshua, but a pretty woman, as pale as me, wearing a fancy hat with feathers, sat there first. She called Joshua darling.

The seat on his other side was taken by a short black man.

Joshua made a little face. I nodded to show him I'd be okay.

I sat on a stool on the other side of the room. Zee sat next to me.

"How old are you, Miss—"

"Dulcie. Just Dulcie. I'm twenty, Miss Zee," I lied. "Is there going to be dancing?" I asked, though there was no room with the piles of books, magazines and papers cluttering most every surface.

Zee laughed. "Oh, Dulcie, honey, no. What did Joshua tell you this was? We're here to share our latest scribblings. Speak our hard-fought-for lines into the air. Not a single step and nary a hop."

The short black man stood up, welcoming us all, joking about everyone.

"That's George. He runs the *Harlem News* and writes satirical novels. His wife is like you."

"Irish?" I asked. I wanted to know what satirical meant.

Zee laughed. "White."

I'm not, I wanted to say, but Joshua said I was.

"Is she white?" I nodded at the woman leaning in close to Joshua, waving her arms around, sounding like Queen Mary from England. Her bangles clattered, ash from her cigarette at the end of a long holder went everywhere.

Zee looked at me funny. "Very."

"Darling Zee!" Queen Mary called.

Zee waved. "Very, very. And so is Godmother." Zee discreetly indicated the woman with tissue-paper skin, dressed in layers of cream lace that went up to her chin and spilled down over her feet. She could be Queen Mary's grandmother.

The old woman gave me a quick smile, then paid attention to everyone else. Listening, asking gentle questions in a posh movie accent.

"Godmother," Zee said, waving at the old woman, "is kind to many of us starving writers."

Zee wasn't starving. I knew hunger: bones sticking out, hair falling out, eyes too big. No one here was starving, what with their fancy clobber and factory-made cigarettes.

"No hooly-gooly, please, darling," Queen Mary said.

Godmother's lips thinned. "She's making up words now," she said, so everyone could hear.

Zee's lips twitched. I bit my cheek to not giggle.

Queen Mary continued talking and waving her bracelet-clinking arms as if Godmother hadn't said a word.

Why did they hate each other?

Zee looked from the two white women to me, like she thought we belonged together. I bit me tongue to keep from saying, We don't.

They weren't trash or confused or Irish or Australian. They had grammar and jewellery and most likely automobiles, fur coats and houses too.

They weren't the only ones at odds. The air crackled with everyone's opinions of each other. If I had safety matches I could set it on fire.

Joshua leaned back in his chair, his long legs stretched to the side of the small table stacked with papers, and started to read.

His voice was low but clear. It tickled my ears, making me think about things he'd whisper to me. I blushed.

All eyes were on Joshua, especially Queen Mary's. I twirled the ring on my finger but no one saw.

Joshua's story was about working on the boat and white people being mean. Listening was like being back onboard with the waves and the ocean spreading out forever. Almost I felt the floor move.

I reckoned he really was a writer.

It was true, I supposed, that people had been mean, but I'd been lost in loving Joshua, and everything was so much better than Surry Hills—fresh water, food every day, learning words and places—it hadn't mattered.

When he finished, we clapped.

Beside me Zee nodded. "He's improved a lot."

The tall black man with the crooked tie wanted to know about unions on the boat. Were there protections for labour?

The older black woman complained about the missing sense of place. What did it smell like? What were the sounds? Did the air taste like salt?

It tasted like salt out on the deck, but in the mess hall it tasted like cooking and sweat.

They talked about his choice of voice, of pointy views, of cymbals, and words I'd never heard. I stopped listening, daydreaming about dancing at a nightclub because we hadn't been to one yet.

Godmother talked about hearing the steady beat of Africa in his words. Zee rolled her eyes, but the old woman didn't see.

The other readers were dramatic, standing up, waving their arms, putting on voices.

I bit my lip not to giggle. Zee did too.

"The year is 1972," the short black man with the cigar began, loudly.

No, it's not, I wanted to say. It's 1932.

His story was about flying automobiles and underground homes. It didn't make sense.

I wondered if it was hooly-gooly.

● ● ●

Joshua took me to a rent party at his best mate's. His friend at the door wouldn't let me in. If his friends didn't like me, would Joshua send me away?

"No room for Miss Anne."

Why did they keep calling me that?

"She's light."

"Ain't no one that light."

"She's my wife."

"If it was just me, but ask Wash what happened last night."

"She's not like that," Joshua said. "She's poor, from the Caribbean." Joshua looked at me, then at his friend. "She's no Miss Anne."

"My name's Dulcie."

His friend shrugged. "Can you lend—"

Joshua reached into his pocket, slid money into his friend's hand, who nodded his thank you and opened the door. "Fats is on the piano tonight. If anything goes down it's on you, not me."

"Sorry, sugar," Joshua whispered, pulling me into the crowded room of people dancing, screaming, laughing.

Joshua was greeted by most everyone with big handshakes and hugs.

In the Hills, you could go away years, return, and the men would barely nod a greeting.

They looked me over a touch too slow. One woman sucked her teeth. My cheeks burned.

"She's light," Joshua said too many times.

They couldn't see my Irish, just my white.

In the Hills no one was white. We were Irish—Catholic like me or Proddys—or Poms or German or Italian or Aborigines or Chinamen.

I was white now. I was the only one in this room who was.

They didn't have to say they didn't want me. They felt the same as Tiny Bruce, Johnno O'Rourke and Tommy Newton did about me and Joshua being together, but they wasn't loud about it.

I decided not to mind, stretching my mouth into a smile. Soon the thumping piano music made that smile real.

Joshua swung me into his arms, jammed in amongst the other dancers, moving me like he'd taught me on the boat.

We fit together. His smile echoed mine.

He kissed me. It was the first time in public. I grinned. He wouldn't chuck me now.

"What do you think, Dulcie baby?"

"Of the kiss? It were dead good."

"Child! Of this party, of Harlem?"

"It's…" He'd taught me so many words and not a one was right. "I love it."

He squeezed me tighter.

"Is this jazz?" I shouted.

His smile went wide. "Sure is."

● ● ●

Joshua whistled as we walked home, his arm around me, though it wasn't cold.

"No one thinks I'm black."

Joshua smiled. "Not yet, but they will. You'll learn."

I liked that he was talking about the future, our future.

A couple strolled by. The man lifted up his tall shiny hat. Joshua lifted his smaller grey one in return.

"Is everyone filthy rich in America or just in Harlem?"

I never saw him laugh so hard.

When he recovered he kissed me. "It's the poorest neighbourhood."

I couldn't believe that. "But your house! It's a palace!"

We were on his street now.

"See this house?" He turned me to a tall house, much like his parents'. He pointed to boarded windows on the second and third floors.

"We're the richest family in the poorest neighbourhood. Striver's Row is crumbling. Hardly any of us left with money. The Crash hit Harlem hard."

I wanted to ask what the Crash was.

"Look at the garbage piled up there. And over there."

I'd never seen streets that didn't have garbage in them.

"It's as poor here as your Surry Hills."

"It never."

"It isn't," Joshua corrected. "It is."

"But the clothes! No one dresses like that back home."

"People here care more about appearances, but the poverty goes down as deep. Harlem is suffocating on poverty and race prejudice."

Race prejudice. I would look it up in his dictionary.

"But you're not. Your family isn't."

"Not so far."

● ● ●

I saw it after that. The toe-raggers on the street begging, folks with raggedy clothes sleeping in the park, rats almost as big as in the Hills. Not as many though, and none at the Irvings'. Mrs Irving wouldn't allow it.

I snooped.

Stood in the corridor, my ear pressed to the door, while his daddy sat quietly working, ignoring them, and Joshua and his mama went mean at each other.

"Are you saying she ain't light enough for you?" Joshua asked. The *ain't* was to poke her.

"Joshua Percival Desmond Irving, that is not the point, and you know it. She's country."

"She's from the biggest city in Australia. She's never seen a cow."

"You know what I mean. How could you have married someone who hasn't heard of Shakespeare, of Toussaint L'Ouverture, of Frederick Douglass?"

"She's Australian. No Australian has heard of L'Ouverture or Douglass."

"That's as may be, Joshua. How could you marry such a wretch? She's not even pretty."

He hadn't. We weren't married. We were just wearing rings. Though I thought the baby in my belly counted for something.

"To break your heart, Mama. I went out and found the ugliest, trashiest gal I could and married her. Is it working? Is your heart broken yet?"

That's why Joshua brought me here?

To hurt his mama?

I sank to the floor as if all the blood and air had left my body.

I was nothing to him.

He was going to throw me over. I couldn't go back to the Hills.

"Jesse's country," Joshua said. "I've never seen Otis so happy."

"Don't talk about that woman. Not in my house."

"Cheer up, Mama. Think how light our children will be."

I heard a sound almost as loud as a gun going off. I jumped up quicksmart, acting like I was on my way from the kitchen, but I was pointed the wrong way.

When Joshua slammed out, his mother's handprint was red on his cheek.

He grabbed my arm, led me to his bedroom.

"Was that true?" I asked, though I'd sworn I wouldn't. "You brought me here to hurt your mum?"

"You heard that?"

I nodded. He wasn't denying it.

"Do you even like me?"

"Course I like you, Dulcie. You're my girl."

He kissed me, soft and warm, his hands sliding around my waist. "You're my girl, Dulcie. For always."

"Your ugly, trashy girl."

"No, sugar, you're beautiful. I was messing with my mama."

"Tell me about Otis," I said to stop myself crying.

"I told you, my favourite brother. Best person in this world."

Joshua was my best person. Where was I on his list? Was I even above his mama?

I pushed him away, touched my stomach. "There's a new best person on the way. Our light-skin bub."

Joshua kissed me harder and whispered the sweetest things.

He was everything to me; but to him I was a stick to prod his mama. I wouldn't cry. I would figure out how to stay.

He nicked off a few days later.

● ● ●

Joshua didn't say goodbye. He left a note, on top of a pile of books he expected me to have read by the time he returned, told me to stay out of his mama's way, what to call the baby if he weren't back as soon as he'd like, and signed off with love.

He wouldn't be here for the baby?

He wouldn't be here for me?

What did he think was gunna happen? His mama wanted to cut me.

I swore I wouldn't cry.

I did.

•••

Once my tears were dry, I went down to the kitchen to talk to Eula. It was where I spent my time when Joshua was writing, helping Eula, staying out of Mrs Irving's way.

I'd helped Aunt May clean and cook for her boss. I knew kitchens.

Eula was a good 'un. She said I might as well be useful.

Eula was who I'd asked what saditty meant.

"That's someone who thinks they're better than everyone else."

I'd smiled. Mrs Irving surely did.

Eula told me about the family.

Joshua was the baby. He did whatever he wanted. He was the missus' favourite.

"Even now?"

Eula nodded.

Allen worked too hard doctoring.

"Missus thinks his wife acts like she's Queen of Harlem, dragging him out at all hours when he should be sleeping. No babies yet. Missus says that's as well because she wouldn't mother any better than a cat."

"What do you think?" I asked.

Eula laughed. "Missus and Augusta got more in common than not, is what I think."

Eula gave me the look that meant, You didn't hear me say that.

Marguerite wasn't married yet, though it wasn't for lack

of offers. Prettier than any of the nightingales at the Cotton Club. Kind too. But Eula wished she'd stop doing that dangerous lawyer work down South.

Otis worked on the trains. He was mechanically minded. He and Joshua were thick as thieves. Eula wished the missus would forgive him.

"What'd he do?"

"The missus doesn't like his wife."

"She doesn't like Augusta neither."

"Not like that. Thinks she's trash."

Just like me, but she lets me in the house. "Why though?"

Eula shrugged. "Missus has her ways."

"Does Joshua nick off a lot?"

"What now, child?"

"Does he go away without warning often?"

"He's a restless one. He was that way as a child. He always comes back."

I wanted to ask Eula if she was sure.

"How old are you, child?"

I hesitated.

"Truth," Eula commanded.

"I'll be seventeen soon but I told Joshua I were twenty. I didn't want him to think I'm a baby. You won't tell him?"

"Not my business."

I thought everything here were her business.

Eula wouldn't tell me about her own family. Though she asked about mine.

"No family," I said, deciding that life was over. "I'm an orphan, me."

Did I know about policy? she wanted to know. Numbers?

I shook my head.

"Tell me three numbers under ten."

"Seven, two, eight."

Eula wrote them down. "We'll do a combination."

She taught me how to make scones. She called them biscuits, which they weren't never. Not even a little bit sweet. Tasty though, melted in my mouth. She said the secret was grease, which looked and smelled like lard.

● ● ●

The day Joshua left, Eula told me, "You'd best be moving on, child."

"Not ready to go to bed."

She shook her head.

"Not to bed—out of the house, out of Harlem. You're white."

I wanted to contradict her but Irish didn't mean anything here.

"It's not the place for you. You could get Joshua in a heap of trouble."

"I would never."

"Yes, you would. No matter what you meant to do."

"You want me to nick off?"

"It would be best. Missus wants it. If you don't go on your own she'll make you."

Why had Joshua left me?

"She doesn't wanna see the bub?"

"What now?"

"The baby."

"You're with Joshua's child? Well." Eula kept kneading. "Well, well, well."

I watched the muscles in her arms stand out. Kneading is hard work.

"Tell me three numbers."

"Nine, one, four."

She repeated them.

"Give the missus the news when Marguerite's here."

• • •

I avoided Mrs Irving till then.

Eula let me know when Joshua's sister was coming.

I made sure I was in the hallway as Marguerite arrived. She'd been away in the South, lawyering. She had bags and a big coat but I flung meself at her before she'd undone a button.

"I'm Dulcie, Joshua's missus."

She hugged me hard. I wasn't good at it. My ma wasn't much for hugging.

"Pleased to meet ya—you. Joshua says you're the best sister."

He never.

"I'm his only sister."

Mrs Irving glided down the stairs, icy cool like.

"Dulcie was about to leave us," she said.

"You're gunna be an aunt," I burst out, touching the wee mound of my belly.

"I am? A baby! Well, you can't be leaving then, can you? I'm going to be an auntie! How wonderful."

"Very," Mrs Irving said, but if her word were a knife, I'd've been bleeding.

• • •

Marguerite gave me clothes. She didn't think Joshua had adequately provided for me. I looked that up after. Adequate. Provide.

"Joshua thinks I can be black like you."

"He does, does he?"

She put makeup on me, to give my eyes and lips some sparkle, she said. It itched.

"What do you think?"

"People see what they want to see."

"That's what Joshua said. Tell me about Otis."

Marguerite smiled. "He's dandy. Jesse too."

"But they never come here?"

"Mama's in a snit because Jesse's not like us. Mama's colour struck."

I'd no idea what that meant.

"Mama's been worse since the Crash. Most of our friends lost everything. She's scared."

I was scared of losing all this too. Me and Mrs Irving were the same. She'd hate that.

But unlike her, I'd been poor, I'd been hungry. Didn't want that ever again. Especially not for the baby.

"Is Jesse like me?"

Marguerite laughed. "Oh, Dulcie."

I was getting used to it. My knowing nothing amused everyone, except Eula. "Well, is she?"

"Yes and no," Marguerite said.

• • •

Marguerite took me out on the town, said she was teaching me to be a respectable Negro woman. Seventh Avenue was crowded with Harlemites promenading, clustered on corners, laughing and gossiping, young men commenting on all the women walking by—"Pay them no mind," Marguerite instructed—and tourists gawking—"And them neither."

It was dark already, the air crisp, and the neon lights glowing. There was music everywhere, dancing out open windows from gramophones, or emerging from guitar-playing men, sitting on stoops with upturned hats to collect coins.

A grim old man with a white beard, veins pulsing on his neck, stood on a wooden box and shouted about sin. "The end is—"

"—a long way off! Let's party!" a young man shouted to the laughing, back-smacking approval of his friends.

"Should we darken my skin?" I asked.

Marguerite looked at me like Mrs Irving did. "No, we should not."

"So how—"

"It's about how we style your hair, how we dress you. How you walk, how you talk."

I nodded but I couldn't never move all elegant like Marguerite or talk like her neither.

"Look at the whites. Compare them to the Harlemites."

I watched a white couple weaving their way past the people lined up to buy tickets to the movies. The man in a tall hat, the woman in a satin gown. They seemed bothered.

"Well?" Marguerite asked.

"The whites've got ants in their pants."

Marguerite laughed. "They're shaky in their own skins."

"I don't walk like that."

"No, Dulcie, you walk like a farmer."

She slipped her arm in mine. "Match my step. Speak like I speak—how I speak out on the town, not how I speak for Mama. You talk too much like that, we might as well give up."

She blew a familiar kiss at two black men gliding by. "Those are Selma's brothers. I've known them since they were babies."

Selma was Marguerite's closest friend. I hadn't met her yet.

"Light steps, Dulcie. Walk lighter, walk taller."

Lighter, taller, I told myself. I stumbled. Marguerite giggled.

"Girl," she said. "Relax. Tread light. Don't clomp. You don't have no glide at all."

She waved at another couple.

"You know just about everyone," I exclaimed. "More than Joshua even."

"I'm a lawyer. Everyone needs me."

Marguerite smiled at young boys, running past, chasing a ball. "Their mama won't be best pleased. Sway your hips, land softer on your feet."

"Why does everyone keep calling me Miss Anne?"

She burst out laughing,

"What?"

Marguerite was hugging herself, crying. "I'm sorry," she gasped.

"I make Joshua laugh too."

"It's an expression, like ofay. It means you're a white gal."

"Oh," I said, feeling dim all over again. "Why are there so many white people here? I thought Harlem was—"

"The Capital of Black America?"

I nodded because I'd heard Joshua and his friends say so.

"It is and it isn't. This is Black Broadway, Seventh Avenue. This is where we promenade."

Marguerite nodded at three women passing, arm in arm, in fancy clobber and shiny lipstick.

"Look at the theatres, restaurants, billiard halls, speakeasies, saloons, nightclubs. Entertainment and joy everywhere. Sparkling glass, gleaming chrome, and the hottest jazz on the planet. Negro Heaven!"

I'd never seen folks dressed so fine, automobiles so shiny. In the Hills there were more horses and carts than motor cars. Horse dung piled high in the streets.

"White people come to Harlem because we dance, we sing, jive and strut better than them. We're color, they're grey. We're movement, they're stasis. We're fire, they're ashes."

Marguerite's cheeks were flushed, her hands flying. I wanted to tell her she should be a writer like Joshua.

"Who do you think owns all this? Who owns the Renaissance? The Lafayette? The Cotton Club? Who owns Negro Heaven?"

"Your pa?"

"White people, that's who. Blumstein's is the biggest store and we can't work there, not behind the counters, smiling and selling those fine wares. They charge us sky-high rents, won't give us jobs, and won't let us in the best clubs, excepting as the floor show! Black Harlem? We live here, but it ain't ours."

I wanted to ask her about Mr Irving. He owned their huge house and the funeral home. Eula said he owned an apartment block and two stores as well.

"But why—"

A white man grabbed Marguerite's arm hard.

"Hey," I said.

"What're you doing with this one?" he said, looking at me. "Pretty little white gal like you."

"She's my sister!" I said. "Let her go!"

"Begging your pardon, sir, but my sis ain't white," Marguerite said, being polite, even though he was hurting her.

He wasn't half as fancy as Marguerite. His teeth were yellow, his eyes bloodshot.

"Look at her hair," Marguerite said. "You know she didn't come by those curls any place white."

"White people can have curly hair!" he protested.

"No, sir. Show me a white with curls; I'll show you a coloured passing."

He didn't know what to say to that.

"She sounds British."

"She's from the islands, sir."

"That's right," I said. "Sir."

Marguerite slid from his grasp, kept walking, pulling me along, kicking up her heels. I did likewise, swaying my hips.

I snuck a peek behind. The horrible white man was staring.

"You'll do," Marguerite said. "Just don't leave Harlem. Can you imagine? Us strolling along 42nd Street holding hands? They'd quail. Are they both coloured or both white?, they'd be thinking, how can we tell the difference?"

"I can't," I confessed.

"White people can rarely tell light from white."

"Joshua says being white is a state of mind."

"Hardly. It's a matter of law and power."

"And the colour of your skin."

"Sometimes that too."

● ● ●

Marguerite took me to see her brother, Otis, and his wife, Jesse. They lived in a two-room apartment, up three flights of rickety stairs.

Otis was tall and handsome like Joshua, with an even bigger smile.

"We've been hearing about you." He pulled me into a bear hug. No one in my family had ever hugged me like that. Otis was affectionate and protective mixed together. It made me want to cry.

Jesse sat in a chair by a wall of framed photos. She was smiling, with her hands resting on her belly.

"You're having a baby too!" I exclaimed.

She smiled wider than Otis. She was beautiful, with high cheekbones and big soft eyes. I wanted to tell her. Instead I touched her shoulder.

"No need to be shy. I've been wanting to meet you," Jesse said, pulling me into a hug as warm as Marguerite's. "I hear Mama Irving hates you almost as much as she hates me. I'm too dark, you're too white."

She was darker skinned than Joshua, Marguerite, Otis, than their parents. She was darker than Eula.

Colour struck, Marguerite had said. Now I knew what that meant.

"That's why she hates you? Because you're dark?"

"And poor and not from Harlem."

"I'm trash," I told her. "She said so."

But Mrs Irving let me stay in the house. She thought white and poor was better than dark and poor. It made my head spin.

"Me too." Jesse laughed.

"Whatcha gunna call the bub?"

● ● ●

Mrs Irving unbent after her first grandchildren were born.

Enough to let Jesse, Otis and Ebony move into the third floor.

But not all the way. She spoke to me and Jesse only about our children. She asked for translations of what I said, long after all traces of the Hills had worn away. She recommended

Jesse bathe in lemon juice and didn't speak to her for a month when Jesse laughed.

But sometimes, almost accidentally, she'd look at me or Jesse and smile.

When Joshua returned—from Paris it turned out—he took our baby in his arms and the grin didn't leave his face for weeks.

"Did you name her like I asked?"

I nodded.

"Lisette," he whispered. "She's perfect."

"You've changed," he said, hours later when Lisette was asleep on our bed. "You look like a Harlemite."

My hair was up in a rag the way Eula did, because I'd been helping her in the kitchen. I was wearing Marguerite's scent and her way of walking too.

"You shouldn't've done it," I said. "Dragged me all this way to spite your ma."

"I know," he said. "I wanted to hurt her the way she hurt Otis. I shouldn't have dragged you in. Not without telling you."

He looked at me, and it felt like he was truly seeing me.

"I'm sorry."

I bit my lip to keep from blubbing. I blubbed anyways.

Joshua held me till the waterworks stopped.

"I'm glad," I said, between sniffles. "I like your sister and your brother. Jesse, Eula and Zee too." Better than my blood family, not that that meant much. "I like Harlem. I love our baby." I loved Joshua too. "But you shouldn't've done it."

"I'm glad too."

We held hands.

"I'm a proper Harlemite now."

He laughed. "Close enough, sugar. We won't ever leave."

ABOUT THE AUTHOR

JUSTINE LARBALESTIER is an Australian-American author of eight novels, two anthologies and one scholarly work of nonfiction, many essays, blog and Instagram posts, tweets, and a handful of short stories. Her most well-known books are *My Sister Rosa*, *Liar* and the *Zombies Versus Unicorns* anthology which she edited with Holly Black.

You can find her on Instagram @DrJustineFancyPants.

• • •

FROM *GOLDEN STATE*

Isabel Quintero

• • •

THE PART WHERE
MARLENE FIRST SPEAKS.

My father and tíos with bloody hands. That is the first memory I have access to. It was my birthday, and I was turning four. I remember a red dress, swollen with crinoline and satin, the kind my parents would have bought at the Chino swap meet on a Sunday after mass. The kind I would've begged for, because the shape of the dress made me feel like one of the dolls my dad was always bringing me from his long trips away from home. The hard plastic dolls with movable arms and legs, eyes that opened or shut depending on whether the little baby was lying down or up and about. About five feet from the bloody mess of a dead pig that my father and uncles were cutting through, I watched my tío Jorge carve a smile into the pig's throat. A horrific version of the ones I'd seen spread on the faces of cartoon pigs. *Pero la niña*, my dad says looking worried. This is my first slaughter. *¡A la verga pariente! Si estuviéramos en el rancho ya nos estuviera ayudando*, Tío Reynaldo, Marlene's favorite tío (second cousin really) teases his youngest primo. But we are not on the rancho, we are in my backyard in Riverside. My legs were so slow to move that I believe I turned into one of those dolls my dad brought me. My once alive arms and legs froze in the upright position. I wasn't able to look away. My large, unblinking, brown eyes opened wide enough to take in every inch of the butchering. That memory, that scene, now reminds me of *The Anatomy Lesson of Dr. Nicolaes Tulp* by Rembrandt—a careful dismembering of a life by hungry hands. A delicate procedure. But that's a more recent connection. Before, I associated that memory only with the last squeal heard before the silence; before carnitas. Back when my tíos made clear their disappointment for the way their youngest brother was raising his American-born daughter—pobre y delicada.

THE PART WHERE THE NARRATOR TELLS YOU A BIT ABOUT LA MARLENE, THE MAIN CHARACTER IN THIS STORY.

The girl in this story does not speak Spanish very well. She doesn't really speak it at all, but her tongue lolls its way over ñ and rrs, hoping to land on correct pronunciations. It dips its tip in accents twice removed. The girl in this story calls herself Mexican even though she was born in the United States. She calls herself Chicana. She calls herself American. She calls herself whatever she wants to, because she doesn't believe in borders or other people naming her. The girl in this story is brown. Brown like her father. Arched eyebrows and freckles like her mom. Small brown eyes like the great-uncle she's never met, whose voice she's heard only on the telephone and through letters. The one who lives in a ja-calito in a pueblo whose name her mouth trips over when she tries to pronounce it correctly. Her mom's favorite uncle with the peacocks and incense. She has her grandmother's thick brown hair and her great-grandmother's sternness. She does not smile on command. Her grandmother didn't, her mother doesn't, and neither will she. The girl in this story could give a fuck what you think and less fucks about the labels you think she should adorn herself with. She doesn't care if this makes you uncomfortable. She is not here to make you feel good.

THE PART WHERE THE NARRATOR GIVES YOU A SYNOPSIS.

Marlene is about to embark on a journey. She has just found out that her father has another family he's kept hidden—in the same damn state. The same fucking state, but up north. Can you believe that shit? Dude kept another entire family in Northern California.

Marlene didn't know what made her look up her geneal-ogy on one of those find-your-ancestors websites. But you know how sometimes you do things almost without think-ing, because it's like your subconscious is guiding you, leading you to some higher truth? Well, she was high, and luckily so, because when she saw that her father, Doroteo Hidalgo, was recently divorced and had a son, she felt the weight of everything on her shoulders. Had she not been high, she would've lost her goddamn mind. Marlene calls her carnala del alma, her good friend Loli, and says, *Read this shit.* Loli does. Both of them fall silent. You don't say jack shit, because there are no fucking rules for this. But like I said, Marlene is about to embark on a journey to find her brother. She's going on this trip with Memo, her best friend. Loli would be going too, except she's too busy getting ready to move into her dorm in a college far, far three states over in Texas. Marlene has tried not to think about what Loli's departure means for their friendship. She is not so naive as to think that it will stay the same, but how far apart they will drift is hard to predict. Besides Memo, Loli Williams has been her closest friend since first grade. But unlike Loli, and to the disappointment of her parents, Marlene doesn't have a Plan for the Future. Or a plan they approve of. In any case, Loli has her shit together and Marlene doesn't, and maybe that's a good thing, because if she did, she wouldn't have time to look for a long-lost brother she didn't know about.

First, she has to pick up Memo, who is about to get out of jail for what will turn out to be the first time. They don't know that yet, though. They won't know that for a long time, so maybe we shouldn't even talk about that. Maybe we should worry only about the immediate future. The one that ends with hope.

Marlene thinks about Memo as she packs burritos, clothes, weed, supplies, and music.

THE PART IN WHICH THE NARRATOR TELLS YOU ABOUT WHEN MARLENE THREW A BRICK AT MEMO'S HEAD, SPLITTING HIS EYEBROW AND LEAVING A PERMANENT SCAR.

When she was about four years old, Marlene threw a brick at Memo's head. It wasn't an entire brick. At least she doesn't think it was a whole brick, just a large chunk of one. They were playing in Memo's backyard, and their parents were inside making ceviche. It was a sweltering day in Corona, the next city over from Marlene's. Probably August, when the heat feels like it will never leave and so your parents turn on the sprinklers for you to run through and cool off. That is to say, it was a perfect day to be a four-year-old in this particular backyard. And this was true until Marlene threw the brick. There is no consensus on the "what" of the argument that led Marlene to reach for what had been left behind after Memo's father had built a planter for his wife's herb and chile garden. Memo argues that Marlene just picked up the brick out of nowhere, because she knew he wouldn't fight back. Marlene claims that Memo said something about throwing like a girl (in her memory they had been playing catch), so she did. In any case, the brick left Marlene's hand with enough force to split his eyebrow. Memo was a bloody mess while Marlene stood there, frozen by what she had done. But only for a moment. In the next second, she ran to help her screaming best friend, using her hands and her shirt to try and stop the bleeding. The crying and screams had signaled to their parents to rush outside.

I'm sorry. I'm sorry. I'm sorry. I'm sorry. I'm sorry. Marlene couldn't find other words.

Memo's mom ran inside to get a rag for the blood. She said they'd have to take him to urgent care.

Marlene's mom yelled at Marlene. *Why? Why? Why?*

I'm sorry. I'm sorry. I'm sorry.

The parents threw the kids in a car and drove; Memo's mom in the back seat, still putting pressure on her son's wound. Something she would always do. Marlene was in the back seat, too, her bloody little hand interlocked with Memo's, making sure he was still there. That she hadn't got rid of him.

Marlene doesn't remember all of it, mostly just the part where she threw the brick and the part where she held his hand.

She thinks about this from time to time when she and Memo hang out. And even when they don't, because that's how guilt works. He likes to joke about it, pointing to his scar, *'Member this?*

She does. The scar is still there. His right eyebrow sports a bald spot. A sort of bootleg, much-less-magical scar than the one that Harry Potter has. Or perhaps more Biblical. Á la Cain, but a different kind of chosen one. On occasion Marlene still holds his hand to make sure he's still there. Though the last time she reached for her best friend's hand was through a glass partition during visiting hours in the correctional facility where he was being held. He was still there, even if she couldn't really touch him.

Memo will be a part of this adventure. This is also a love story. Don't overthink it.

THE PART WHERE MARLENE ASSESSES HER FATHER THE LIAR.

My father is a liar. Like his father before him and before him and before him. The machismo runs deep in this familia.

I use the word cautiously. *Familia.* It is a blood bond. A latching of ancestral memories, habits and traumas. I imagine this link like hooks connecting us to one another. Or maybe like fish caught by the same rod with thousands of lines and hooks, our mouths just ripping at different angles.

But like I said, my father is a liar. Like his father before him.

THE PART WHERE TÍO REYNALDO'S MOM DIES AND THE KITCHEN IS FLOODED IN TEARS AND TEQUILA.

Tío Reynaldo sits at the kitchen table. Tío Reynaldo is crying. Into his hands. It is a waterfall. Our feet disappear and the tears engulf our ankles. We slosh our way to him but it takes a while to reach him. We don't reach him. We won't ever reach him. My mom had burned a tortilla and the kitchen is still smoky. The comal is still on. The smoke seeps into the tears around our ankles. We can barely see through the smoke. Tío Reynaldo is obscured. He is a shaking mass. A silhouette. The kitchen is a mess. Tío Reynaldo is a mess. He left Penjamo, Guanajuato, where his family moved after they left Sinaloa, thirty-five years ago. In Penjamo they make a famous tequila. When he is sad, Tío Reynaldo drinks that tequila. Maybe it is not tears around our ankles. Maybe it's tequila. Maybe it's both. It could have been twenty years, since he left. It could have been ten. It could have been a hundred. It could have been yesterday. It doesn't matter, because the point is that he left. And now both his parents are dead. They are dead. Both of them. He is an orphan. He hadn't seen them since he left thirty-five years ago. When you don't have papers, when you leave your country without papers, without permission, when you enter the United States without permission, when you make this place your home, you are immediately orphaned. You lose people. On the journey. En el otro lado. En este lado. You lose people. This country takes things from you. It wants to know how bad you want to stay here. There are ultimatums. Es chantaje. If you love me, this country says, you will stay. You will not leave me. If you love me, you will cry. You will work, here. If you love me, this country says, you will let me have my way with you. This country is often a bad lover. Or maybe just a very selfish lover.

THE PART WHERE MARLENE LEARNS THE TRUTH ABOUT HER FATHER.

Ready to Find Out Your Family History?
    Yes.
    Enter your father's name…
    Entered.

    Enter his place of birth…
    The same rancho my abuelitos were born on in Sinaloa.

Enter his birthday…
Same as his dad's.
Click on the branch.
Click.
…

There must be another man with the same name. The same birthday. The same place of birth. My father would not have another family. He is not recently divorced. He could not have other children.

This is what keeps replaying in Marlene's head. The moment she found out her father had another family. A wife and a son. A son and a wife. A wife that is not named Laura. Marlene's mother is Laura. Laura has one daughter with Doroteo Hidalgo. Marlene. They do not have a son. But here, on this website that promises to reveal your genealogy, your family history, Marlene learns that Doroteo Hidalgo has a son named Diego. He is almost two years older than Marlene—nineteen years old. Doroteo Hidalgo, from Riverside, California, was recently divorced from one Lourdes Hidalgo. Marlene is confused. And then she is not. In a short amount of time, she has learned much family history.

Things become painfully clear. Now, there are answers to questions she forgot she'd been asking since she could speak: Why are you gone for so long? Why won't you be here for Christmas? Who is the boy in your wallet?

Marlene confronts her father. And then her mother when she learns that her mother has known the whole time. Things do not go well. These things never do. There is crying. There is blame. Doors are slammed.

MARLENE GETS TO THE JAIL AND WAITS OUTSIDE FOR MEMO BEFORE THEY TAKE OFF.

She's watched this happen in movies many times. At the end of *Ocean's Eleven* when Tess is waiting for Danny. Or when Karen waits for Henry in *Goodfellas*. But neither of those films really encapsulates how it feels to wait for someone you love to be released from a cage.

Tío Reynaldo had been put in a cell, once, too. This was years before the government steadily detained children, when the country hung on more faithfully to the facade of justice and equality. His face was never blurred in an article written by a journalist clamoring for humanity. Or attention. No, Tío Reynaldo had had too much to drink one night and had been pulled over. Bad luck. Mala suerte, her mom had lamented. He was eventually released and did some community service. Marlene was very young then and couldn't fully understand what it meant to be locked away. Not the way she does now.

Fuck, it feels like I've been waiting forever. Marlene wipes sweat from her eyebrows again. When she looks at her watch she realizes she's been waiting for only twenty minutes.

It's hot outside the jail in Banning. The desert greedily and mercilessly absorbs the California summer. Even this early in the day the sun is not kissing her skin as much as biting it. If her mom were here, she'd have a hat on and would probably be reapplying sunscreen. Most likely she'd go back in the car and turn on the a/c, because her pale ass doesn't tan, just burns. Marlene, who takes after her dad, likes the way her skin turns a deeper shade of brown in the summer when she spends most of her time outside, swimming or hiking or walking her dog. She still applies sunblock though. Too scared of melanoma and its cousins. Marlene once looked up skin cancer because her mom had a strange mole on her arm and she was panicked it was cancer. It wasn't. Nonetheless, Marlene went down a skin cancer rabbit hole, self diagnosing until Memo pointed out that her mom had always had that mole on her arm. *When we were little and your mom walked us to the library, I remember holding her hand and thinking how it looked like a tiny crescent moon and star,* he'd said. So, it couldn't be cancer. Memo was good at reassuring her when she'd overthink.

Finally, Marlene can't take the sun anymore and gets in the car. The a/c has barely started cooling her off when Memo walks out the door. Memo, tall, brown, dimpled, and smiling, plastic bag in hand. Marlene can't make out what he's saying, some joke, probably, because he's laughing. She opens the door and runs to meet him.

Why you cryin'? Memo jokes.

Shut up, Memo.

Kali Uchis's "Ridin Round" starts playing on the car stereo as Memo closes the door to the car. As if on cue. As if to get the road trip started.

What up, mija? We going on an adventure or what?

Just like that, Marlene is at home and free and all her problems seem solvable. That's what Memo does. He gives her the possibility of possibility.

She hands Memo a paper sack with his favorite snacks: a bag of mango chile paletas, several Reese's, Baby Ruths, Takis, and two ice-cold cans of Arizona Green Tea with Ginseng.

You really do love me, Memo teases.

He hands Marlene a mango paleta, pops one in his mouth, turns the radio up, and jokes *Let's go, before they know I'm missing.*

Neither of them bother looking back at what they're leaving behind as they race towards the 10.[1]

THE PART WHERE YOU LEARN ABOUT HOW TÍO REYNALDO AND MARLENE ARE REALLY EXTENSIONS OF THE SAME LONGING.

Decades before, upon first arriving in the United States, Tío Reynaldo had taken that same 10 all the way to Florida. He made stops in Phoenix and El Paso. Then San Antonio and New Orleans. He was a young man. His parents were still alive, and he still believed in the American Dream. He didn't fear deportation as much as he does now. But then again he was young and doing all the things young straight men were supposed to do. Working long hours for women and fun times. He had picked up English easily and quickly learned to use it to his advantage, especially with White women who found him "exotic." Women who asked him to talk to them in Spanish in bed. He figured it was quid pro quo, because they were both fulfilling a need. Though his need was more natural than their racist fantasy.

Reynaldo (this was before anyone called him tío) drank and slept and smoked and danced his way through the Amer-

---

1   For those non-native Californians: whereas in most parts of the US folks say, "Interstate 10" or "I-10" when talking about an interstate, in California we usually say, "the 10" or "the 91" or "the 405" aka "the freeway from hell."

ican Southwest that summer in 1985. He and his primo, Chico. Chico, who missed the rancho too much to stay in el norte but left him a little black-and-white TV and most of his cologne collection. This was Reynaldo's favorite summer. No parents. Single. No major responsibilities. Just a 1964 cherry-red Plymouth Valiant taking him and Chico from the Pacific to the Atlantic.

• • •

Perhaps this is where Marlene gets her incessant desire to roam. To be a pata de perro. She has always been this way. And he has always been this way—itching to wander, and aching when forced to stay put.

When she was little, and when Tío Reynaldo would come down to visit, he would take her on long drives through back roads throughout Southern California. She got to know the Inland Empire, her home, this way. Tío Reynaldo would take her on the winding roads through Reche Canyon to look for wild donkeys.

He had brought up the wild donkeys in conversation and Marlene didn't believe him.

There are no wild donkeys in Southern California, tío, she said to him.

Why would I lie about that? Tío Reynaldo rolled his eyes.

I don't know why. You just lie sometimes. It runs in our family.

Ay Marlene. Come on. I'll prove it.

So they jumped in his old red-and-white Ford truck and went in search of wild donkeys.

The sun was setting and the hills on both sides of the road that twisted itself from Colton to Moreno Valley began the shift from dry desert landscape to being awash in the gold disappearing from the rays of sun that made the dangerously dry shrubs and brush seem magical before darkness completely overtook everything.

Marlene almost missed the little donkey standing by a fence post. Tío Reynaldo pointed it out with a whistle.

Ay, mira. There's one.

Sure enough, Marlene looked up and sees the little brown donkey. When she looked a little to the right, she spotted about ten more donkeys, just chilling. That evening she and Tío Reynaldo spent a few hours driving through Reche Canyon and San Timoteo Canyon Road. This was a favorite pastime of theirs; wandering to just wander. No aim, no specific X.

They were quite the pair. Tío Reynaldo in his fifties, brown hair thinning, thick-rimmed glasses, stylish clothes that didn't reveal that he spent most of his days changing oil or cooking kale and sweet potato mash or whatever the ever-changing and ever-hungrier American palate asked for. Then there was Marlene in her teens. T-shirt and jeans, flannel and jeans, blouse and jeans. It would be a sweet story to say that they enjoyed each other's company from the first time they met, but that would be a lie. While she didn't dislike Reynaldo, Marlene was indifferent during his visits.

She found him mostly tolerable and a little annoying because he was one of those adults who always made cheesy jokes and tried to be pals with the kids. It wasn't until Marlene saw Tío Reynaldo playing the accordion and singing Ramon Ayala that he became more than an annoying uncle.

During a cold autumn night that smelled of birria and leña, years ago when she was a child, at a birthday party for a cousin visiting from Mexico, Tío Reynaldo transformed from tolerable and annoying, to someone fascinating and worth knowing. Marlene had already been sent to bed but someone's aunt's sister had brought out a guitar and was belting out Chavela Vargas with such sentimiento that Marlene knew, having never even been in love yet, what heartache felt like. What that particular sadness was. By the end of the song women were openly crying, and men were drying their eyes. Marlene sat in awe of what music could do to a person.

But when Tío Reynaldo picked up the accordion and started playing what could almost be called "the other" Mexican national anthem, "Tragos de amargo licor," that was it. She learned that there was something more sincere in that man than she had believed.

Marlene thought of that moment whenever she hung around Tío Reynaldo and any time she'd go see him perform in bars or lounges she probably shouldn't have been at. She thought about that moment now as the familiar tune poured from the radio and she turned the volume up without thinking. The song was midway through and Ramon was singing about how much like a coward he felt for drinking his feelings away. Tío Reynaldo and Marlene joined voices as San Timoteo Canyon got darker and the high beams were turned on.

But they stopped singing as they came up to some of the citrus groves that still dot Redlands. What the high beams highlighted was almost unbelievable to Marlene—a herd of donkeys amongst orange or lemon trees, though it was hard to tell which was which in the dark. There they were, cute and dumb looking, caught infragante and mid-chomp, oranges in their mouths, their eyes full of surprise as the high beams shined on them.

This is why Marlene loves Tío Reynaldo: because he's always shining a light on dark places, always teaching her that the unknown isn't always frightening. That the unknown is simply that, unknown, and that if we are not cowed by not knowing, or by money, that if the fear doesn't keep us safe and sound at home but instead drives us to know, leads us directly into temptation, well then, we are constantly changed and can create change. We are never done growing and, therefore, he adds, we never stop being young.

That's how I keep my youthful glow, Tío Reynaldo joked.

No pos wow, Marlene responded. *I just thought it was the not having kids and being single.*

That too, he added. *But mostly it's the curiosity.*

Haven't you ever been curious about that?

About what?

Being married and having kids?

Ay, Marlene, let's not talk about sad things, he said and quickly went back to the wild donkeys.

THE PART WHERE YOU LEARN ABOUT MEMO'S AND MARLENE'S FAMILIES.

There are people who are born to sit. To stay in one place. Whose eyes do not wander, much less their minds. Who live in fear of the unknown and who haven't been curious since the first time they fell off a tree and never attempted to climb again. People who when there are no real, physical, fences or barriers, will quickly erect imaginary ones so as to reassure themselves that they are safe. However, that assurance is also imaginary because there is no such thing as real safety. That is an illusion.

Memo and Marlene have parents who are both from this country and from another country. They do not come from families of sitters or stay-putters. They come from a family of fence hoppers and explorers. Some, like Reynaldo and Marlene, are patas de perro and were born to wander. Others left out of necessity. In either case, their families are a mix of people who can come and go as they please to the country of their birth and ancestors, and of people who are trapped by an inefficiently run and racist system. A system that has enacted laws and physical structures that get people killed for simply trying to leave poverty and reunite with family. Marlene had an uncle die in the desert and Memo had a cousin drown in a river, crossing to El Gabacho. Marlene's father was born on a rancho in the middle of Sinaloa and her grandmother finally left her husband, Marlene's grandfather, for good when Doroteo was four years old. His brothers, much older than him, were already in Gilroy with Reynaldo, working in restaurants and a tire shop. Trying to find their place in their new country. Marlene had visited the left-behind grandfather a few times in her childhood. The once big man lived small in a haunted apartment in Celaya, Guanajuato. He was old and lonely, and rarely left his couch, where he watched courtroom dramas and telenovelas with his cat, Petra.

To have families in two countries is to have part of yourself missing. Perhaps this is not the case with people who, if they have the money, can jump on a plane and cross borders without fear. But for much of Memo's family, and some of Marlene's, leaving is never easy. Marlene thinks about how her tía in Sinaloa will never see the house her brother built or come over for Sunday carne asada. How she has cousins she will never be close to, because their parents decided to have sex in a different country and this country is a closed border for most Brown and Black people—and Brown and Black people is exactly what their families are made of.

So maybe this journey to find her brother is not just about her father lying and confronting that lie. Maybe this journey is also about keeping all the family you can together, desperately gathering them like sticks to start a fire. Because, often, that's what it feels like we are: the kindling that keeps everything warm in a country made of water.

ABOUT THE AUTHOR

ISABEL QUINTERO is an award-winning writer and the daughter of Mexican immigrants. She lives and writes in the Inland Empire of Southern California. *Gabi, A Girl in Pieces* (Cinco Puntos Press), her first YA novel, was the recipient of multiple awards, including the California Book Award Gold Medal and the Morris Award for Debut YA Novel. She is the author of the chapter books, *Ugly Cat and Pablo* (Scholastic, Inc.) and *Ugly Cat and Pablo and the Missing Brother* (Scholastic, Inc.). In 2016 Isabel was commissioned by The J. Paul Getty Museum to write a nonfiction YA graphic biography, *Photographic: The Life of Graciela Iturbide* (Getty Publications), which went on to be awarded the Boston Globe Horn Book Award. Most recently, *My Papi Has a Motorcycle* (Kokila), her latest book, earned the Southern California Independent Booksellers Association Award.

• • •

HARD TO SAY

Sharon Morse

• • •

There's so much I don't remember about where I was born. Venezuela is just a few hazy scenes in my mind, so loosely tied together that they feel like dreams instead of memories. I don't remember my school, except for the sweet, smiling face of one of my preschool teachers. I don't remember our home, except for the balcony off the living room where I could feel the tropical breeze brush across my cheeks and whip my hair into a halo around my head. I don't even remember the language—my first language. It, too, got lost to the haze of dreamlike memories.

My sister remembers it all. She was ten when we moved—old enough for her memories to stay intact. I had my sixth birthday just after we got to the States.

I try not to get jealous as I walk into the kitchen to the sweet smell of cinnamon pancakes and the sound of Clarísa speaking Spanish on the phone with our grandmother. My sister laughs and asks how she and our grandfather are doing. I know enough Spanish to figure at least that out.

"Morning," my mom says as I pull out a stool next to my sister.

"Morning," I answer.

Clarí stands from her stool and walks to the other side of the kitchen, like the two words that Mom and I uttered are disrupting her enthralling conversation.

Mom slides a plate of cinnamon pancakes in front of me, swimming in butter. It's a tradition my mom has insisted on since my last day of kindergarten, when she accidentally knocked the cinnamon over and it went flying into the batter. We deemed it meant-to-be and carried on the tradition ever since. "You know," I say. "I'm almost seventeen. You don't need to make me special last-day-of-school pancakes anymore."

"I'll be making you last-day-of-school pancakes all the way through grad school, kid. Deal with it."

I pop the top off the syrup bottle and pour it all over the pancakes. "So, you're going to travel to wherever I'm attending college and make pancakes on a hot plate in my dorm room?"

Mom raises an eyebrow. "FedEx," she says, dropping the pan into the sink. "Or you can always go to school close enough to come home for pancakes, like your sister."

I laugh as I cut into my pancakes, letting the syrup run down through the layers. "Moms be crazy."

"You laugh at me now," she says, wiping down the countertop with a kitchen rag, "but you're going to miss this when you're all grown up and I'm too old to trust around an open flame anymore."

"Nah." I pop a bite into my mouth, savoring the butter and cinnamon and maple syrup on my tongue. "I'll put you in an old folks home way before that."

"Valentina. Have a little respect for your mother." Mom swats at me with the kitchen towel. "At least make it a nice one—a retirement community for active seniors. With a pool for water aerobics."

I laugh. "Deal."

Mom does that mom thing where she watches me like I'm going to grow up and leave the house if she dares to look away.

"I still have senior year, Mom. There will be more pancakes ahead of us."

"I know." She purses her lips and nods.

"Oh, God, are those tears?"

"No!" She hisses and turns away to start washing the dishes.

I cram another bite in my mouth and chew around my smile while Clarísa paces the length of the kitchen with the phone pressed to her ear. Her mouth moves a mile a minute in perfect Spanish.

Even though Spanish was my first language, now I have trouble piecing together even the most basic conversations. I can understand bits and pieces when someone speaks slow enough. But I can barely find a response with two hands and a flashlight unless it's sí, no, or gracias. It happened without even realizing it. One day it was just…gone. I can't even tell you when.

Dad shuffles into the kitchen and puts an arm around me, giving me a good squeeze along with a loud kiss to the top of my head. "You ready for junior year to be over?"

I nod and swallow, my mouth full of pancakes. "So ready."

"History final today?" He sits on the stool next to me.

"And I have to turn in my final art project," I say, nodding to the canvas on the kitchen table, a landscape of Texas blue-bonnets and an old hill country barn to showcase perspective. I brought it home last night to work on the last few details.

"You'll nail that one, no problem. And I call dibs once it's graded. I want to hang it in my office."

"Deal," I say, smiling into my pancakes.

"Dad, Ita wants to talk to you." My sister holds the phone out to him. Ita and Ito became my grandparents' names when Clarí was little and couldn't say Abuelita or Abuelito. Everyone thought it was adorable, so of course it stuck.

Dad's smile falters as he grabs the phone. "Hola, Mamá," he says, but he walks toward his office before we can hear anything else.

"Is everything okay?" I push my plate toward my sister, and she takes my fork.

Clarí shoves a huge bite into her mouth. "So good," she mumbles to herself. "I don't know," she finally says when she's done chewing. "I tried to ask how things were going, but she wouldn't tell me much other than the weather."

I try to ignore the tightness in my chest. Clarísa's managed to stay close with our grandparents, but when you don't speak the same language anymore, staying close isn't so easy.

Clarísa sighs and runs a hand through her thick hair. She takes after Dad, with darker skin and hair. I try not to be jealous of that, too. My mom is beautiful, but Dad definitely has the good hair.

Dad's words float down the hallway, and we lean back on our stools, trying to hear more. He talks way too fast for me to pick up any of the words, but I can tell by his tone that something's up.

We both turn our heads to Mom, who starts tinkering around the kitchen, cleaning surfaces that are already clean.

"Mom, what's going on?" Clarísa asks.

Mom just shakes her head. "Let your father tell you, okay?"

My sister and I look at each other as all sorts of scenarios run through my head. I search her eyes, wondering if I'll find the answers there, but it's clear that, whatever this is, Mom and Dad are shielding it from Clarí, too.

We both know the situation in Venezuela has been getting worse. We've all held our breath, waiting for tiny crumbs of updates from American news outlets. Over the past year I've followed some of the protests on Twitter—what I can make sense of with Google Translate, anyway. The worse the situation has gotten, the more the mainstream news has reported about it. Every time another update comes about the violence, the lack of food and medicine, the millions of people leaving the country daily, the strain it's putting on Colombia and Brazil, I can feel the tension in the house rising. It's in the set of my dad's shoulders, the tight smile on my mother's face, the hushed, late-night conversations in Spanish.

It's hard to imagine it's the same place where I would stand on that breezy balcony and watch the colorful birds fly by.

Dad shuffles into the kitchen, a smile on his face like nothing is wrong.

"Dad, what's going on?" Clarí's voice breaks and she swallows.

Dad sighs and runs a hand through his thick curls. "Things in Caracas are…not good. You know already."

I know that my parents have been sending money to my grandparents for several years. And I know that's why Clarí had to say no to half the schools she got into in favor of public, in-state tuition, and that there was no discussion of buying me a car on my sixteenth birthday like so many of my friends. But as things have gotten worse, sending money has turned into boxes full of grocery staples, basic household supplies, and finding an American doctor who could help us send Ito his heart medication.

"Is everything okay with Ito?" Clarí asks.

Dad nods and sits down on the stool next to mine. "Everyone's fine. We just...have some news." He turns on his stool to face us. "Your mother and I have been working with an immigration lawyer for several months. After this election, we asked her to fast-track everything. We weren't sure if it would work out, so we wanted to wait until we knew for sure to tell you girls."

"And?" Clarí asks.

"The lawyer called yesterday. We've got their visas."

"They're coming to live here?" I ask, leaning on my elbows, like if I get closer to Dad, he'll have to tell me more. "With us?"

Dad nods.

"When are they getting here?" Clarí asks.

"Day after tomorrow," he answers. "Plane tickets are already bought."

Clarí's eyebrows practically retreat into her hairline. "That's really soon." But there's a lot in that sentence that she's not saying. Mainly, how long they've been hiding this from us.

"Where will they sleep?" I ask.

"In your room," Mom answers. "You can move your things into Clarísa's room, and you two can share while she's home for the summer."

I nod. My room is bigger and the bathroom is attached.

That's obviously where they should sleep. But Clarí and I have never shared a room. We haven't shared much, really. I love my sister, but we're not like TV sitcom sisters. We aren't really close, but we don't really fight, either. We're just...sisters. I've felt helpless for so long, watching my parents deal with this. At least I can do something to help.

"I can move my stuff after my last final today," I say.

"I'll help," Clarí adds.

"Are you going down there to help them move?" Ito and Ita are in their eighties now. There's no way they can pack up all their things by themselves.

Dad gets up from his stool and paces across the kitchen. "A few years ago, it was pretty simple for a citizen to sponsor a family member, especially elderly parents. But these days it's...different." I can tell there's more he wants to say. He clenches his fists at his sides like he's trying not to get worked up into an angry rant.

"What do you mean?" I ask.

"The lawyer recommended I don't go there right now."

"But why? How are they going to move all their things?"

"Don't be so naive, Val," Clarí says. "Venezuela's on the travel ban list."

I slink back in my chair. "I thought a judge blocked that?"

"Temporarily." She pushes the rest of the pancakes across the counter. "But they're still detaining all kinds of people at the airport for no reason."

"But Dad has his citizenship now."

"Hasn't stopped them from bothering anyone else."

"Clarísa," Dad says. "Enough."

I look back and forth from my sister to my dad. "So, who's going to help them?" I ask, feeling more helpless than ever before. All our relatives in Venezuela moved back to Argentina, where Ita and Ito are originally from, several years ago. And most of our family friends have spread across the world. Everywhere from Miami to Lisbon to Singapore.

"No. They have to leave pretty much everything behind. Walk away from their home. Your sister is right. It won't be easy for them."

"No," I say as I poke at the last bite of pancake. "I guess not."

• • •

Mom nudges my shoulder in the middle of the night—at least it feels like the middle of the night. I groan and roll over in the new twin bed Mom got at Costco. We set it up yesterday, across the room from Clarí's. We didn't have time to prewash the sheets, so they still smell kind of like plastic.

"We're leaving for the airport," Mom says in a whisper even though everyone in the house is now awake. "We should be back in a couple hours."

"A text message would have been sufficient," Clarí whines.

"Oh, no," Mom says. "I want you girls up and dressed when we get back with your grandparents. You want them to arrive to two zombies just shuffling out of bed instead of their lovely granddaughters? What kind of welcome is that? Come on. Up." Mom flips the lights on and we both groan. I throw my hand over my face, letting my eyes adjust.

"Evil, evil woman," Clarí mutters, rolling back over.

"Uh huh," Mom says, like she's proud to bear the name. "Just get your butts up and throw on some decent clothes. No pajama pants."

"Eeeevil." Clarí kicks the covers off her bed, seemingly in protest.

I sit up and yawn. "Do you need to pee?" I ask my sister.

"Yeah."

"Well, go now. I'm going to take a shower."

"No."

"Okay, but once I get in there, you're gonna regret that you didn't go before I got in."

"No," she groans again.

"Suit yourself." I stand up and make my way to the bathroom in the hallway that used to belong to just Clarí, but now is ours. I'd just go take one last shower in my bathroom, but it's pristine with a new shower curtain and everything. Mom will kill me if I mess it up.

Halfway through my shower, there's a bang on the door.

"I have to peeeeee!" My sister's voice rings out over the running water.

"What did I tell you?" I yell back. "Go use Mom and Dad's!"

Sharing a bathroom is going to be so much fun.

• • •

The squeal out of my grandmother's mouth when we open the front door is so loud, I'm surprised the neighborhood dogs don't all start barking. She beckons to me and I can't help but run to her. She grabs my face with both her hands and searches my eyes. I smile as she talks to me; some I can understand, some I can't. Something about how I'm beautiful, and my guess is how grown-up I look. She hasn't laid eyes on me since I was little, so I'm sure it's as strange to her as it is to me. She squishes my cheeks again before crushing me to her chest, and I can't help but let out a laugh. I sink into her hug and breathe her in. She smells like peppermint and the stale cabin air of an airplane. And she's so thin that I worry my hug might crush her.

I get one more cheek squish and a kiss before she wipes her lipstick off of me. She turns to Clarí and does the same thing—sweet words and kisses until all her lipstick is on Clarí's cheeks instead of Ita's lips.

I turn to Ito to say hi and he gives me a shy smile. He looks so much older than the photos we have of him. His hair is whiter, and the skin around his eyes and mouth is more wrinkled and weathered. I lean in to give him a hug and he puts his long arms around me. He kisses the top of my head the way Dad always does and holds on just a little longer without saying anything. Ito is a man of few words. Right now that suits me just fine.

Dad tells us all to grab a suitcase—in Spanish, but with his gestures it's easy to understand what he's asking—as Mom leads my grandparents inside the house. I watch as Ita walks inside, keeping a hand on the underside of Ito's elbow, like he needs the stability. Dad says something I don't understand and points down at the threshold, and I realize he's telling them to watch their step.

After I set the last suitcase down in their closet, conversation in Spanish floats down the hallway from the kitchen and I follow the sound. When I walk in, Clarí is showing Ita around the kitchen, which Mom and Dad just updated a bit last year when all the nineties-era appliances started dying one by one. Ita runs her hand along the stove, saying something complimentary. She looks up at Dad and says something else, and everyone else laughs. I get from the way Dad looks half amused and half affronted that it must be a joke about him—his cooking I guess? But it's hard to know for sure.

• • •

My stomach growls as I walk into the kitchen, surveying a mess of flour and dishes.

"Your dad decided to help your grandmother make empanadas, so it's taking a while," Mom says. "Of course, it doesn't help that he's spent most of the time telling your abuela that she's doing everything wrong."

I laugh. "Isn't she the one who taught him how to make them?"

"Yes, but of course, he says he's perfected them over the years and so she should do it his way now. I swear, that man." She says that every time Dad is being stubborn, which is at least once a day.

We finally sit down to eat in the dining room with a huge spread in front of us. There are empanadas as far as the eye can see. Dad informs me that the ones on the white platter are his and the ones on the platter with the flowers are Ita's and I'm to eat some of each and compare.

Mom bites her lip, visibly resisting the urge to say something. I catch her eye and she shakes her head, mouthing *I swear*.

They're both delicious, but the table erupts into arguments about which one they prefer. Or at least, I think that's what they're talking about. The conversation flies back and forth so fast that I barely catch a word.

Clarí jumps up and puts a napkin ring on Ita's head and she laughs. When I hear her say "La reina," I finally get the joke and laugh along with everyone else. Clarí has crowned her the queen of empanadas.

But it only gets harder to keep up after that. The conversation flows easily between everyone at the table, with laughter and raucous interruptions and gestures. Ito says something to Dad, then looks at me with a smirk on his face. Dad throws his head back and laughs right from his belly.

I look from Ito to Dad to try to figure out what they're saying about me. Clearly it's amusing. When I don't get a clue from them, I look to Mom, but she's laughing too.

Dad finally catches his breath and looks to me with tears in his eye from laughter. "¿Recuerdas ese viaje?" he asks me.

I blink and try to decode what he's asking me. If I remember something. But what?

"Of course you don't, you were so little," he says, switching back to English for a second at my confused look. But then he switches right back, turning to Ito, and I'm back to not knowing what in the world anyone is talking about.

I grab another empanada off the tray—one of Ita's, because they are better by a slim margin—and pick at the braided edge of the pastry as the conversation goes on around me.

● ● ●

I sleep in the next morning, because it's summer and I can. But when I go to get some cereal around noon, Ita and Clarí are in the kitchen. My sister is chopping something green while Ita gives her directions, motioning with her fingers to chop it in smaller pieces.

"What are y'all making?"

"Chimichurri," she says without looking up. "To go with dinner tonight."

I walk across the kitchen and lean over to hug Ita.

"Buenos dias, Tinita," she says, giving me a kiss on the cheek. Tinita was always her nickname for me, which makes me smile. Mom and Dad used to use it, but since we moved here, I preferred just Valentina or Val, so I'd asked them to stop. Now I kind of wish I hadn't.

"Buenos dias, Ita," I tell her. I hope my pronunciation was okay. I'm trying to keep my mouth open more when I pronounce my vowels. I read that online somewhere. Hopefully it's not terrible advice, but it is the internet, so who knows.

I gesture to the pile of herbs Clarí is working on with Dad's best knife. "Can't you just make that in the food processor?" Dad always does. Chimichurri is an Argentine sauce we keep around all the time; Dad probably makes a batch every week or so. I had to laugh when it started to become trendy and we suddenly saw it everywhere. But Dad says no one ever gets it right. That Texans always add cilantro.

Apparently he doesn't either, according to Ita.

Clarí shakes her head. "Ita says that's, like, sacrilegious. Hand-chopped is the way to go."

"Si," Ita responds. "A mano."

"She was mad that Dad doesn't have a mortar and pestle, but I think that's way too old-school for him." Clarí laughs.

"Can I help?" I ask, but it looks like they're almost done.

"You can grab the oil." Clarí nods toward the pantry.

I grab a couple of bottles, not knowing which one they want to use. To be honest, I never paid much attention when Dad was making it before. Cooking was always more Clarí's thing. "Which one?" I ask.

Ita takes the bottles from me and inspects them. After taking a taste from each one, she settles on the olive oil and sets it next to the bowl already full of the chopped herbs, garlic, and red pepper flakes.

Clarí scoops up the parsley and dumps it in the bowl. She asks Ita something in Spanish that I don't understand, and the two of them start talking. Their voices get louder, gestures more pronounced. They both take food pretty seriously.

"Mírame," Ita says, pointing to the corner of her eye. Watch.

She perches the bottle of oil in one hand, thumb over the top to control the flow. With the other hand she begins to lightly stir the mixture as she slowly streams in the oil. It's just stirring, but she does it with flair. Like a *Top Chef* contestant sprinkling salt in the pan.

Clarí has more questions. And the two of them are off again on their intense foodie conversation. The more excited they get, the faster they talk. And the faster they talk, the less chance I have of picking up even a single word.

While they're distracted, I stick my finger in the bowl and then lick it.

It's good.

Better than Dad's.

I lick off the rest and forget about the cereal I came for. I just wipe my hand on a kitchen towel and go back to my room. The chatter continues in the kitchen. Ita and Clarí don't even notice I've gone.

● ● ●

"What crawled up your butt?" Clarí asks as she comes into the room. "We were having fun and you just left."

No, you were having fun, I don't say. "Nothing." I grab my clothes out of the drawer and try to stomp past her to take a shower, but she grabs me by the shoulder.

"Just tell me what you're mad about." Clarí always wants to hash things out as soon as they come up. Doesn't she get that some of us like to stew in silence for a while?

I squeeze my eyes shut, trying to breathe through the lump rising up in my throat. "Just let me by."

"No." She steps out wider to block the doorway.

"Ugh. Clarí. I really don't want to talk about this right now. Especially with you."

"What does that mean?"

"It means you couldn't possibly understand what this is like for me. You and Ita are, like, best buds."

"We were trying to include you. You're the one that walked off."

"Well, you were doing a crappy job."

Clarí doesn't have a clever retort to that one. She leans against the door frame and I take my chance to squeeze by her.

I finally let myself cry once I shut the bathroom door, hating that Clarí can probably hear me anyway. Of course she doesn't understand why I'm upset. She hasn't lost what I've lost. She hasn't had to grieve for something she doesn't even remember having. I let the steam fill the tiny bathroom, fogging up the mirror while I hide away and let the water wash away the tears.

● ● ●

I wipe the sweat off my forehead as I walk in the back door. Walking over to my friend Amy's house in June was clearly a terrible idea. I always forget how hot ninety-something degrees is until summer comes around again. But I needed to be out of this house for a while, and I didn't feel like bugging Clarí for a ride after our fight yesterday.

When I step into the kitchen, Mom looks up from sorting through a bunch of plastic bags spread across the table. "Oh, good. There you are."

"I went to Amy's," I say. "What is all this?"

"Oh, I took Ita to the art supply store to get some things so she could paint." She pulls a tube from one of the bags. "We dug your easel out of the box under your bed," Mom says. "Hope you don't mind."

I shake my head. "No, it's fine." I survey the stuff spread over the kitchen table. Mom even got out the old tablecloth I use when I paint at home.

My tabletop easel is set up, and there are several new canvases stacked on the counter. "You guys didn't need to buy all this stuff. I have plenty of paint and brushes she can use."

"Ita likes to use oil paint," Mom says. "She says that you don't use the same type of brushes for that."

"Oh." I guess that's true. I never thought of that. No one at school uses oils. Someone asked our teacher about them once, but she went on a tirade about the smell of turpentine, so no one ever asked again. Plus, from what I know about it, you have to wait a whole week for one layer of paint to dry so that you can work on top of it again.

I can't even wait all the way through a YouTube ad without hitting Skip.

Ita walks into the kitchen holding an old box. "Come," she says to me. "Sit."

"Me?" I point a finger to my chest. I look from Ita to Mom. The timing of all this—and the encouraging smile on Mom's face—makes me wonder if Clarí said something to Mom about my little meltdown yesterday.

"Sí." She sits down at the table and opens the box. It's full of old pieces of paper. I sit beside her as she sifts through them all, not really searching for anything. Just looking. The box is full of beautiful images—magazine clippings of beautiful people or clothes or buildings, those *National Geographic*-type photos of animals or places. They're all really old, the paper crinkled and starting to yellow. She reaches a stack of photographs, and I recognize me and Clarí when we were little. Ita passes it to me with a smile.

"Que linda," she says. How cute. She waits for me to look at the photo, then grabs hold of my cheek and gives it a pinch.

"Ita," I laugh, brushing her hand away.

A photo of a beach catches my eye as she sifts through the stack. I reach for it as Ita puts it down next to her and I know I remember this place. The way the palm trees lean in, surrounding a half-moon bay. And the color of the sand. Red. Almost like Texas dirt.

"That's Playa Colorada," Mom says over my shoulder. I didn't even know she was standing there.

"It's in Venezuela?" I ask.

Ita nods. "Sí."

"I've been here before?" I ask, sure that I must have.

"Te acuerdas?" Do you remember?

"Sí. Me acuerdo," I say, impressed at my on-the-fly conjugation. But I know we learned that one in junior high Spanish. "Or, I think I do."

Ita tells me the story, or starts to tell it to me, then switches to telling Mom. Her way of asking her to translate.

Mom tells me that we went there a few months before we moved to the States. That I had so much fun that day, I didn't want to leave. As she talks, some of the details start to fill in.

"I think I do remember. Clarí buried me in the sand..."

I look at Ita and she nods, smiling. Her smile makes me remember more than the beach. I remember the whole day. Playing with the other little kids, sitting with Ita in the hammock Dad strung up between the palm trees, Dad hacking away at a coconut, trying to get to the sweet water inside. Mom digging that giant hole in the sand so that Clarí could bury me up to my neck.

Ita digs through the rest of the photos, and there it is. A photo of just my head, sticking out of the red sand and Clarí holding the shovel with an evil grin.

Ita grabs the first photo from the tabletop. The one with the pretty palm trees. She says something to Mom, nodding to me.

"She wants you to paint this."

"Me? I thought she was the one painting," I say to Mom.

"I show you," Ita says to me.

And she does. We start with the sky, blending blue and white into thin, wispy clouds on a sunny tropical day. The oil paints blend together so easily, and you can keep blending the colors even after you've spread them on the canvas. It takes some getting used to, but I love the feel of it.

After a while, I don't even notice how long, Mom leaves us on our own. The second I realize she's gone, my chest gets tight with worry. What if I have a question, or Ita asks me something and I don't understand? But after blending the reds and browns and yellows to mimic the bright color of the sand, I realize we don't actually need words right now. I pay attention to the way she changes the angle of her brush, and I watch as she shows me how to get the texture of the sand to translate onto the canvas.

The brushstrokes are their own language.

ABOUT THE AUTHOR

SHARON MORSE was born in Caracas, Venezuela, to an Argentine father and an American mother. When she was six, her family moved to her mother's hometown of Houston, Texas, where Sharon refused to speak a word of English until her first bite of a Shipley's donut. Sharon still lives in Houston with her husband and four kids, three of whom have disabilities. When she's not busy advocating for her kids or writing, you can catch her in the kitchen where she runs a small cake business. Find her online at sharon-morsebooks.com and on Twitter @sharonmorse. This story is her first publication.

• • •

CONFESSIONS OF AN ECUADORKIAN
Zoraida Córdova

• • •

Dear Yoda,

I know that my last entry was dated three years ago on the first day of 7th grade after Horacia Móntes kicked me out of our Spice Girls cover band, but it's me, Paola, and I'm back. Hi. Hello. Hola. It would take me a hundred years to tell you everything that's happened, and my mom says I can't buy another diary until I finish this one. So, in the words of Inigo Montoya, "Let me sum up."

The rest of junior high school sucked. Not the cool kind of suck like being a vampire (I'd make a very good vampire by the way). It sucked in a way scientists haven't even begun to find a solution for.

7th grade: I lost all of my friends because Horacia said I had no talent and was not as pretty as she is. That's fine. I mean, it's not actually fine. She called me a Really Bad Thing★ that

I had no idea was an insult. Now that a few years have passed, I'm glad she broke up our friendship. My cousin Gabriela who is one year older than me and way cooler than Horacia said that I shouldn't surround myself with heifers who will put me down. Did you know that a heifer is a cow? I definitely didn't until today. (That's not what Horacia called me.) Anyway.

We also moved into a two-family house. My mom, grandma, tía Felicia, and ñaño Toto pooled all their money and bought our very first house. Mom, grandma, Lily, and me live on the first floor. Tía Felicia, her husband, and my cousin Ronaldo are on the second floor. My mom's youngest brother, ñaño Toto, lives in the basement but he's barely ever home because he works in Manhattan and his commute back to Queens Village is over an hour and a half. Anyway, that's the only good thing about that year, even though I have to share a room with my little sister.

8th grade: I graduated junior high and became a citizen of these United States! I wish that my mom had told me to, I don't know, brush my hair for the photo? I already hate my nose and that my hair is too in-between curly and straight. Now I have a certificate that says I'm an American and a photo that says I was hatched in a Dagobah swamp.

Getting your citizenship kind of feels like getting your graduation diploma. It's the same shape and cardstock with gold cursive letters and some official-looking seals. Except, when you graduate school, you know what you're getting right away: more school. But when you pass your citizenship test, what do you do? Do you keep studying and memorizing dates and the names of presidents? Horacia was born here and she doesn't even know that Pocahontas was a real person or that Puerto Rico is a commonwealth of the United States. She didn't have to take a test because she was born in Brooklyn a decade after her parents immigrated from El Salvador. Lately, I'm not exactly sure what it means that I'm an American citizen.

I was born in Guayaquil, Ecuador. My little sister, Lily, was also born there, but we moved to New York when I was five and Lily was ten months old. Lily has no memories of Ecuador. I have some but they're fuzzy. I remember a big house and a metal swing in our backyard. I remember a mango tree and a goat that died after a rainstorm. What am I supposed to do with those memories now? The way my mom talks, we're never going back. It's confusing and I don't have anyone to talk to about it. I know if I asked my mom she'd say she can't afford to be confused because she has to work. Sometimes I wish we were the kind of family that talked instead of the kind of family that swallowed our real feelings like bad medicine.

My citizenship diploma, or whatever it's called, is in a blue leather folder in my closet. We should really get a fireproof safe because what happens if it burns or there's a flood or I lose it? Does that mean that I have to go away? Do I have to sit in that office all over again staring into the face of an angry old Italian man who scowled so badly he looked like the time I over-boiled a potato?

I just don't know, Yoda. Mr. Johnson made us keep a reading journal and I think it helped me write better essays. If only I could figure out a way to get straight As in life. Maybe writing down everything that lead to My Cousin's Big Fat Disaster Quinceañera will make this tight feeling in my chest go away.

Finally, 9th grade rolled around. Everyone made a big deal

about starting high school, but I didn't get what the big deal was other than everything being terrible. I think I have to break it down into further sections.

9th grade—Part A: Remember my ex-best friend Horacia? Well, she came back and started dating MY COUSIN RONALDO. So she was here all the time. Et tu, Ronaldo?

It's not his fault, I guess. Gabby says boys only think with one thing, but she didn't exactly say what that thing was supposed to be.

The sad part is that I used to love Horacia. There was a time we were inseparable. We went to P.S. 95 together. Her mom used to send me an extra pupusa stuffed with cheese and chorizo for lunch because my mom didn't have time. When I got my period at ten, I thought I was dying. My mom was at work and I was too embarrassed to tell ñaño Toto, so Mrs. Móntes gave me a pad. I'd had a nose bleed earlier that day and thought the blood was going the wrong way. But then after she called me a Really Bad Thing* I realized my friendship with Horacia was over. How can you give someone a friendship bracelet one day and then decide you hate them the next? How can you be "part of the family" one day and then ignore them in class?

Gabby says not to worry about it. That life is long and I'll have amazing friends one day. But what about the parts of life I'm living now? For instance, a few weeks ago when I walked down the halls at school and Horacia shoved into me and called me "Ecuadorkian." It felt like being punched in the face. I wanted so badly to not let it bother me. But I gave in. I hit her and got my first detention ever.

To top it all off, my ñaño Toto said I had to be "the bigger person" and apologize. That words are just words. But he's wrong because I know words can hurt just as badly as any punch.

When she came over, Lily and I had to sit in the living room with Ronaldo and Horacia as "chaperones" because Horacia's mom would only let her come over if they "chillaxed" with us. And if Ronaldo wanted to show Horacia his FIFA World Cup collection (no one wants to see that, Ronaldo) then I had to be in his room, too, like a chastity ghost or something. Ecuadorian parents—Latinx parents really—always have their minds in the gutter. No, not even the gutter. They're where the gutter empties out in a pit of perverted thoughts. I swear that all they think about is sex. Even if you're not having sex. I'm definitely not having sex, but it seems like everyone around me is obsessed with it. My mother and grandmother won't even say the word. They just talk around it. For instance, if there's a boy too close to me at the bus stop, my mom glares at him until he leaves, and dead ass, her eyes bulge out of her head like a scene from Beetlejuice. The first time I invited friends over, she might as well have shined a light in their eyes and swabbed the inside of their mouths for some DNA.

Oh, I have friends now, by the way. We're the weirdos who hang out at the abandoned bus stop across the street from the school.

Anyways, she was dating Ronaldo, so Horacia took over my personal space and we had a Cold War going on over the TV and stereo all summer. She wanted to listen to Britney Spears and I wanted to listen to Green Day. I thought I was going to win this war, but after what happened yesterday, I'm not so sure.

That brings me to 9th grade—Part B: I ruined my cousin Gabriela's quinceañera last night and my family hates me. I did something bad. Like real bad.

It all started eight months before the quince. It was the coldest fall I can remember and the day I met the girl who would become my best friend. Alyssa Aragon was standing at the abandoned bus stop and so was I. The problem was, neither of us knew that the bus stop didn't work. We thought that all the punk and skater kids were there because they were also trying to get home.

There was a particular boy there dressed in a black hoodie and combat boots. Even though he was scowling and SMOK-ING A CIGARETTE, I enjoyed staring at him. He didn't look too much older than me, maybe fifteen or sixteen. He caught me looking and smiled. I felt like something amazing had slammed into me and I immediately became obsessed with him.

Enter Horacia with her two friends in matching new low-rise jeans and the same North Face jacket that everyone in school seemed to have. My jacket and most of my clothes were hand-me-downs from ñaño Toto. I had on an ugly corduroy jacket and boots that were half a size too big so I wore two pairs of socks to make them fit.

Horacia saw me and rolled her eyes. We'd had a cease-fire after the last time she told the Spanish teacher that I didn't speak any English. Poor Mrs. Hunter. She spoke REAL SLOWLY and turned tomato red when I opened my mouth and proved Horacia wrong. She didn't even get in trouble. Then, I left my gum on her seat and she told my mom. We

had to buy her a new pair of jeans. Gabby told me I have to
get better at revenge.

"Hey, freak," Horacia said to Alyssa.

Alyssa didn't look up from her journal. She also has a diary,
but she hasn't named hers the way I did.

"I'm talking to you," Horacia said. "You're a Satan wor-
shiper aren't you?"

Alyssa snapped her notebook shut and looked up. She had
the prettiest oval eyes with long black lashes. Her raven dark
hair reached down to her waist, ending at bright bleached tips.
When she tucked loose strands behind her ear, I could see
that the whole cartilage was studded with glittering piercings.

"Actually, I am," Alyssa said and grinned.

Horacia and her friends stopped laughing. Alyssa stood up
and started speaking in tongues. She shook her body, thrash-
ing her arms around, and flipped her hair over to look like
La Llorona. Then she held her fist out, opened her palm, and
blew invisible dust in Horacia's startled face.

Some of the other kids were watching. The brooding boy
with the combat boots smirked and kept smoking his cigarette. I was ready to applaud and everything.

"Now let me wait for the bus in peace," Alyssa said.

Horacia must have realized by then that Alyssa was not,
in fact, a Satanist. "You do know this isn't a real bus stop?
Dorks." For some reason she thought it was hilarious. I could
see the moment a light flicked on in her head. "The Devil
and the EcuaDORKian."

There was a chorus of "Haha Ecuadorkian" all around us.

Then she and her friends left and I sat there staring at the tops of my sneakers wishing Alyssa really were a Satanist so the ground beneath me would open up and swallow me whole.

"So, this is not a bus stop," Alyssa said. "I just transferred here. What's your excuse?"

"I missed the cheese bus. I've never taken the public one before."

"At this point we might as well walk. I'm Alyssa."

"Paola," I said.

Who knew I'd have a reason to thank Horacia? If not for her, I might not have talked to Alyssa and realized that she was just as lonely as I was. Friendships are forged through tough times. Like Sam and Frodo. Han and Chewbacca. Sailor Moon and the Sailor Scouts.

As we walked home from the bus stop, I noticed a name stitched on the arm of her green canvas jacket.

"Hey is that from *Lord of the Rings*?" I asked. "I've been trying to read the book before the movie comes out."

Alyssa laughed but didn't think I was a giant loser talking about fantasy books. "It's my last name. Spanish, I think. My family's Filipino."

That's the moment Alyssa and I discovered that we were basically the same people. She was born somewhere else and immigrated to New York when she was a kid, just like I did. The only difference is that the school board made her repeat a grade. She used to be fluent in Tagalog, but after she got teased by the other kids for it, she didn't want to speak it anymore, which makes me sad. It almost feels like having to cut off a part of yourself, a tongue maybe, just to fit in. I wish things weren't like that.

Technically we're the same age, but she's one year behind.

She transferred to Queens Village because she was getting bul-
lied so badly at her private Catholic school with girls throwing
literal rocks at her. She has a pretty wicked scar on the side of
her temple where one hit her. Also, she says *wicked* a lot and
I've decided to use it. She also introduced me to this amazing show BUFFY THE VAMPIRE SLAYER. But I have to
go to her house to watch it because we don't have cable and
my grandma would freak out about me watching a show with
witches and vampires.

I don't know what I'd do without Alyssa. She even came
in and helped with Gabby's quinceañera. Getting her to help
was about the only helpful thing I did, really. Three months
before the party, one of Gabriela's friends left without a word.
She just stopped showing up to school and answering Gabby's
calls. I overheard my mom and tía Felicia whispering in the
kitchen that the girl's family got deported and thank God that
it would never happen to us. I spent the whole night thinking about it. How was my tía so sure? When ñaño Toto came
home that night at MIDNIGHT, I asked him why people got
deported. He said that it was when people overstayed their
visas or came to this country without one.

"Did we have visas?" I asked him.

I noticed how tired he looked from his long commute.
Ñaño Toto is really my uncle. He's my mother's youngest
brother. Ecuadorians use the words *ñaño* and *ñaña* for their
siblings. Since my mom leaves for work at five in the morning
and comes home barely in time to eat dinner and fall asleep
while watching her telenovelas, my uncle Toto (Antonio) helps
take care of me and Lily. He's been happier lately, dancing
around to his favorite Freestyle and house music. Not that he

was miserable before but being a social worker for little kids in bad situations really takes a toll on him.

He said, "We did come here on visas. But we were lucky. My aunt Maria and her husband have lived here since 1976 and they were able to send an invitation to my mom. My mom then got invitations for my sisters and me."

The whole thing about invitations was so confusing. It's like being a citizen was an exclusive club. I still couldn't understand why we got lucky or why Gabby's friend wasn't. Suddenly that citizenship diploma in my closet felt different. It was like my permission slip proving that I was allowed to be here forever.

It seemed almost silly to be excited over a party after something like that had happened to her friend. But Gabby couldn't cancel her quince. She was going to turn fifteen and had been planning hers since she was six and attended her first quinceañera. In Ecuador, the party is a neighborhood-wide ordeal. But in Queens Village, they had to rent a hall and there was a limit of people they could invite. I don't think that I want to have one next year. My mom works like twelve hours a day to barely pay the mortgage and basics, why would I want to spend a gajillion dollars on a single party?

Gabby says it represents womanhood and family and blah blah blah. But she doesn't understand because her dad has a job at a bank and she has both parents to take care of her. My dad is in Ecuador. Don't get me wrong. I don't feel like I'm missing my father at all. I have my uncle and my grandmother and my mother. My family is different than others, but they are enough. It would just be nice if my mom didn't have to work so hard. I hope that when I'm older I can get a good enough job to help her so she can just relax.

Okay, yes, I'm stalling because I'm afraid to write about the thing that I did.

When Gabby needed to replace one of the members of her "quince court," tía Felicia suggested Horacia.

"No way," I said.

"Why not?" Ronaldo asked. "I have to dance with her anyway."

Gabby shook her head and smacked her teeth. "Because I don't want her. She's stank and rude."

"She isn't to me," he countered.

"Then you should pay more attention and see how she treats other people."

"Me," I said. "I'm other people."

That turned into a whole fight. But I'm glad that Gabby had my back. I only wish that things had been different and that I hadn't ruined her party the way I did.

Alyssa just happened to be at the house when Gabby was struggling with finding a replacement for her friend. We were going to watch *The Craft*, which we rented at Blockbuster while my grandma was at church. "I can do it."

"What do you know about quinceañeras?" Ronaldo asked her. I don't know why he acted like he didn't check out Alyssa every time she walked into a room.

Alyssa scratched her nose with her middle finger to flip him off on the down low. "I'm Pinoy. Filipinos have these parties, too. Except they're called Debuts and we have them when we're eighteen. Put on a fluffy puke-colored dress and spin around with a guy wearing too much Abercrombie & Fitch cologne who steps on my feet all night. Been there."

"You're hired!" Gabby said.

With Alyssa taking part in all of this, I wasn't afraid to look stupid wearing the puke pink dress. So we practiced and danced around learning all the steps. I can't tell you how many times we listened to "Tiempo de Vals" by Chayanne, or how many dress fittings we had where the seamstress practically turned me into a voodoo doll. But the routine felt nice and I understood what Gabby meant about quinces being about family.

Horacia was PISSED that she wasn't invited to be one of the fourteen damas who made up the court. Why did she want to be a part of it so much? She didn't even like our family. And she was already invited because she was Ronaldo's girlfriend.

Horacia started being meaner and angrier to Alyssa and me when no one was around. But I ignored her because that's what ñaño Toto told me to do. But I don't think that always works. Sometimes people are so unhappy and so miserable with themselves that they have to make others feel the same way.

Last week before the quince, Alyssa and I stayed after school on the Corner. The Corner is what everyone calls the defunct bus stop. Alyssa and I shared earbuds and listed to a scratched No Doubt CD on her portable CD player. Here, my baggy clothes and messy hair fit in because everyone dressed like that. No one made fun of my hand-me-down jeans or shoes. Instead, we all took turns drawing on our clothes with sharpies. I decorated the sides of my pants with safety pins. I drew on the white parts of my bootleg Converse, and then everyone started asking me to do theirs—flowers, Pokemon, the Rebel Alliance symbol. My drawings were actually pretty good. At least, Miguel thought so.

Miguel was the angry boy with the combat books. He's a year older and has blue eyes and a gap between his teeth. I wonder if that's why he doesn't smile much. On his backpack he's got a Puerto Rican flag stitched next to his Metallica patch. Whenever I'm around him my tongue feels like the Arizona desert. Not that I've ever been to the desert.

The other day, I had dropped a *Star Wars* pin from my backpack and he picked it up. He said "cool pin" and I stared at him like he'd just sprouted three heads. My insides felt like a sarlacc beast lived in them, like the one that almost ate Han Solo in Return of the Jedi. I took my pin and ran away. Literally ran. Alyssa teased me all the way to quince dance practice.

Okay, Yoda. I think this is the day everything really started going wrong. I noticed how Alyssa and Ronaldo were finally getting along. The two of them were the best dancers of all fourteen damas and chambelans. I don't know a lot of things, but Ronaldo was look looking at Alyssa the way Aragorn looks at Arwen. Like she's wondrous and made of magical elvish light. I sensed trouble.

When he was packing up his things, I caught him off guard.

"What are you doing?" I asked Ronaldo.

He shrugged and raked a hand through his floppy curly hair. "Packing up? Why are you being weird?"

I rolled my eyes. "No. With Alyssa. I see you flirting. It's not fair to her or Horacia, as much as I hate her."

"I'm not doing anything." Ronaldo scrunched up his face. "Not everyone is your dad."

"Wow, that's rude," I said. For as long as I can remember, any time my father was mentioned, tía Felicia would go off on what a cheating bastard he was and that she was glad he stayed in Ecuador. Most of the time, I'm glad too. My mom deserves the best of everything. But I wonder, can I be mad at him and still find a little part of me that loves him at the same time? Maybe when I go visit next year I'll find out.

"I'm sorry. Things with Horacia are weird. She's always mad at me for not calling her when I get home from practice, but I was tired and had to help my mom do laundry. And she knows if I don't pass Social Studies I'll have to repeat it. But still, that was a low blow."

"I know you're not like that," I said. "But if you like Alyssa, why not just say something?"

Ronaldo glanced around nervously. "Do you think she likes me? I mean, has she said anything? About me, specifically."

"She said you were cute but that you had a girlfriend."

"Why do you hate Horacia so much?" He was serious. He was the cousin I'd grown up with my whole life, who shared his last Eggos and Dunkaroos with me. "You used to be together all the time and then one day nothing. I asked her once and she said you ditched her because you act better than everyone else."

Remember that thing I wrote about from 7th grade? The reason Horacia and I stopped being best friends? Well, I never told anyone until that moment. I took a deep breath.

"She called me a stupid ugly FOB. We were in class and she whispered it to her friends so I could hear it. I didn't even know FOB meant 'fresh off the boat.' I know that as insults go, everyone refers to kids as FOBs. Like that kid from Guyana who just moved over? People call him that and then they laugh. They think it's a joke and it's no harm done. But no one saw him crying in the hallway after and I wanted to say something, but I didn't know how. It just made me feel really shitty."

Ronaldo shook his head and gave me a hug. I hadn't realized how much that had bothered me until then and it was nice having my cousin there. "The other day I was in class and this kid called me a spic because it was unfair that I got straight As in Spanish since it was cheating. It sucks. I'm sorry."

We went home and, he didn't tell me, but he broke up with Horacia that night.

That explains why the next morning Horacia showed up at my house with her mother and asked to speak to my mom. It was the weekend, and my mom's only day off, but she let them in. They said it was important, that Mrs. Móntes was thinking about our family's "well-being" and that she'd want to know about my behavior. See, Horacia had brought over this photo of me. She's obsessed with these disposable cameras and she took one of me at the Corner with Miguel. It was at the exact moment that he handed me my *Star Wars* pin. But because of the angle and the cigarette tucked behind his ear, it looks like he could be handing me anything. Specifically, DRUGS.

"I'm not doing drugs!" I shouted as soon as I shut the door on Horacia's self-righteous, lying ass.

Nothing I said seemed to matter. My mother was yelling about me being one of "those girls" from bad neighborhoods who have no business being around boys. That she watched on a news special on Telemundo how even the scent of marijuana would cause me to become a zombie and ruin my life. As punishment for something I didn't even do, I couldn't leave the house except to go to the quince rehearsals and I was lucky I even got to do that. And they tell me that TV will rot my brain.

I kept the photo that Horacia left behind. Miguel didn't look angry. He was smiling. AT ME. It sparked something in my gut. I didn't care about Horacia or her mom. I didn't care that my own mother didn't believe me. The more I stared at that photo the more I realized I was different than the girl Horacia once knew. I was a good girl, even if it didn't match the definition my mom had. A wild sensation stirred in my heart, waiting to be unleashed, and I knew just where to start.

I asked Alyssa to come over the next day with the supplies I needed. Bleach and pink hair dye. We went down to my uncle Toto's basement apartment because he's hardly ever home. It took five hours, but my hair turned out the exact color of Gabby's quinceañera dress. I stared at myself in the full-length mirror while she looked at the picture he had framed of me and Lily on the coffee table.

"Hey doesn't your uncle still live here?" Alyssa asked.

"Yeah, why?" I asked.

She picked up a stack of papers from the coffee table and handed it to me. I wasn't sure what I was looking at, but it said Astoria Apartments and it had my uncle Toto's government name and someone else's. "Who's David Santos?"

Alyssa shrugged. "Looks like a new apartment lease."

My uncle was leaving us. He was moving out. Why hadn't he said anything to anyone? There was already so much happening that I couldn't handle it. I left the papers there and went back upstairs. There was a slick, hot sensation in my heart that told me things were about to change in ways I wasn't ready for.

The next morning, my mom saw me and freaked out. "Why? ¿Por qué? Why?" She kept saying. Good Ecuadorian girls don't dye their hair without permission. They don't act out, apparently.

"We're going to church," she shouted.

"Why do you care what I do now?" I yelled back. "You're never even home!"

That might have been too much because my mom stopped yelling. Ecuadorians love yelling. It's actually our normal tone of voice. It's how we communicate anger and love and friendship. But mostly anger. So when my mom shut down and turned away, I knew I'd said something wrong.

Ñaño Toto walked in at that moment. He looked flustered and hesitated. "You can't talk to your mother like that, Paola."

I was tired of everyone. I know I shouldn't have said it. But I was mad at him too. What was I supposed to do if he left? Who would I have? Gabby and Ronaldo lived upstairs but they had their own family unit. All I kept thinking was the stack of papers with his new home. He hadn't even told us he was leaving. He'd made this decision already and we didn't matter. I was helpless and my only weapon was my words. Words can hurt just as badly as any punch, remember?

"You're not even going to live here anymore so you can't tell me what to do! You're not my father."

He was too shocked to reprimand me. He never yelled at me. I was more than his niece. I was his friend. His little sister. His daughter. All of those things in one.

It's hard to explain the anger that I had in my chest that day. I could blame everything on Horacia, but I know that I didn't have to say those things to my mom and Toto. I know that there are things I don't understand like why my mom bottles her feelings or why my uncle kept such a big secret from us. I want to understand so much. But sometimes it's easier to just lash out. To let that anger loose. The only problem with that is that now I'm left with the aftermath and I'm not sure what to do.

We kept living with that silence. School and work don't stop just because feelings are hurt. Besides, there was a quince to celebrate, and my mom had already put the deposit down on the dress.

We went to the party. Everyone stared at me. I've been so used to trying to blend in, to make myself small, to watch. I wasn't used to having people examine me like a display at a sideshow. Gabby really loved my hair and her opinion was the most important one that day. I'm glad someone was happy with me because my mom was seething. All my life I thought that she had two modes: busy or tired. But I realized that, until yesterday, I'd never truly seen my mother angry.

My grandmother said I had no respect and "nice Ecuadorian girls don't act like you." But aren't I supposed to be a "nice American girl" now? What does it mean to be Ecuadorian when they didn't even show me how to do it? I'm not the one who packed up all our things, got on a KLM flight, and started a new life. I'm not the one who chose this, so why am I the one who is left to figure it out on my own? What does it mean to be American when everyone we know is an immigrant? Is it the same exact thing? Can I be both things? It feels like I'm just supposed to have the answers to these questions but how am I supposed to figure anything out when it seems to me that communication is not one of the languages my family speaks?

Anyway, we get through the dance like we practiced. The chambelan who escorted me only stepped on my feet once. I think he was my tía's coworker's son. He didn't talk much, which was a relief. The twenty minutes of dancing were the quietest I've had in forever.

But then, it was all over, and I saw him. Miguel. My brain went foggy and all the strobe lights and confetti made me feel like I was in the middle of a music video. Why was he there? His familiar frown split into a smile when he saw me. Warmth spread from my aching toes to my belly and settled right in my chest.

Miguel was starting to walk over to me when Horacia blocked his path and faced me.

"You made Ronaldo break up with me," she shouted over the music.

"I didn't do anything! I told him what you called me."

"You're such a little kid, Paola," she said. "Why can't you just take a joke?"

"Because some things aren't funny. You can't just say things like that and act like you're not trying to hurt someone. I don't know what I ever did to you, but I don't want to be your friend."

The next part I'm not so clear about. I know that in that moment Ronaldo and Alyssa were dancing. He spun her around and they looked happy. Sweet, even. Horacia whirled away from me. I thought that she was going to make a scene, so I grabbed her by the wrist and pulled her. At the same time, she shoved me away.

I should have let go.

I should have done a lot of things differently. I should have tried to understand my mother more. Tried to be a better cousin to Gabby for her quince. Figured out how to use my voice to speak without having to write it down. I should have tried to learn to walk in heels. If I had, then maybe I wouldn't have lost my balance and tumbled right into the five-tiered cake covered in buttercream flowers. I might have saved the cake table from flipping over and landing on top of three other damas, and then in turn, stopped those damas from crashing into a waiter carrying a giant tray of drinks.

Maybe things happen for a reason. Everyone says that but I can't tell what's true or what's an accident. If my dad had never cheated on my mom, would she have wanted to stay in Ecuador? If I hadn't had a fight with my mom, would I have dyed my hair? If I hadn't caused a complete and utter scene I wouldn't have had my Uncle Toto drive me home and I wouldn't have stayed alone in his car while he went to get gas.

I wouldn't have seen his cell phone light up with a message from someone named David that said: Everything will be all right. I love you. You are my life.

I remembered the name on the lease right next to my uncle's. David Santos. David who loved my uncle. David who was the real reason my ñaño Toto was in a better mood. I wonder, what does it mean to be someone's life?

When he got back in the car, I sat with my sticky hands on my lap staring at the car in front of us. He turned on the music—our favorite Enanitos Verdes song. He drove and gripped the wheel tight. He didn't bring up the mess I'd made or what I had said to him about not being my dad. I wanted to take it back, because he is what my father could never be. He was there.

But I don't know how to talk about things that matter. Sometimes I wonder if silence is something you can inherit from your family like dark hair or the shape of your teeth or the nose you think you'll never grow into. I wonder if you can leave the bad things in a country you will maybe never see again. I wonder if I'm too young to think about these things, but I don't know what else I'm supposed to be thinking about when no one talks.

"I was going to tell you about David," Ñaño Toto said. "I wanted to tell you before the others. You know you're my number one person."

"Then why are you leaving?" But I knew why. I had a feeling in my gut. Also, I had read the text message that wasn't meant for me.

"Because I met someone. I love him and we want to start a life together." He looked at me. I made sure that I didn't look away when I told him that I loved him.

We drove in silence all the way home. My mom and grandma and Lily would come home with tía Felicia way after midnight. But for a few hours we had the house to ourselves. We knew that things were going to be different. Or maybe they wouldn't. But no matter what, I'll be there because my uncle will need me when he brings David home to meet the family, and I will be there just like he was for me my whole life.

Get ready for a new school year, Yoda. There's the Halloween dance at the end of next month, and I have to bake a cake to make up for the one I ruined. I have to decide if some friendships are worth saving or letting go. I have to try to teach my family to speak, because now I'm certain of how powerful words can be. It's a whole lot of firsts. I feel like I'm changing, and I don't know if I'm ready for all of it to happen at once. But I can only ever be the girl I've always been. Ecuadorkian and proud of it.

Love,
Paola

ABOUT THE AUTHOR

ZORAIDA CÓRDOVA is the author of many fantasy novels including *Incendiary*, *Star Wars: Galaxy's Edge: A Crash of Fate*, the Brooklyn Brujas series, and the Vicious Deep trilogy. Her novel *Labyrinth Lost* won the International Latino Book Award for Best Young Adult Novel in 2017. Her short fiction has appeared in the *New York Times* bestselling anthology *Star Wars: From a Certain Point of View*, *Toil & Trouble: 15 Tales of Women and Witchcraft*, and *Come On In*. She is the co-editor of the anthology *Vampires Never Get Old*. Zoraida was born in Ecuador and raised in Queens, New York. When she isn't working on her next novel, she's planning a new adventure.

• • •

FLEEING, LEAVING, MOVING
Adi Alsaid

• • •

F or Shmuli to exist, borders had needed to be crossed. Now came another. He had a student visa printed into his passport that told him so, made the move official, despite his trepidation. He would not die on the crossing, there was no risk of that at all. The plane, maybe, but no more risk than anyone took on any given day.

This was merely a matter of paperwork and lines at the airport. This was not like the Syrian border in 1948. His grandmother, a baby then, had wanted to wail for the discomfort of the journey, but a hand had been clamped over her mouth so that the British soldiers, the Lebanese soldiers, the many men out there looking for human beings not allowed to go from one place to another, would not hear her distress. That hand might have almost killed her, his grandmother always said, but it saved her, too. Silenced her into survival.

No such danger for Shmuli, though there had been a moment when his earphones weren't all the way in and he hit
Play before boarding the flight, and someone had cast a dirty
glance his way.

Yes, without mere survival, without that hand clamped
over his grandmother's infant mouth, Shmuli would not be
on that plane, would not be on the planet at all. 1948, nota-
bly, would have ended him, and 1941, too; probably many
other examples could have been dug up before that. Years
when the world would have ended Shmuli's grandparents
or great-grandparents or some other descendant had they
not escaped from one place to the other. The accounts of
many of those years, however, were simply lost. His great-
grandparents had survived 1941 and 1948; they had crossed
away from danger, and so Shmuli existed.

Shmuli, though, did not exist on mere survival. He was a
specific human being, unmatched by any other human being
who was living during his time, or, indeed, any who had
come before. Not in skills, or any particular sort of excel-
lence (although he was a terrific sleeper, and not too shabby
at video games and school), but merely in the specific details
that made him who he was. The way, for example, that after
a meal he pushed himself away from the table, turned parallel to it, and crossed his legs as he digested. He did this only
because he had learned the behavior from his father. His father learned the behavior from his own father, who had done
it only because the dining room where he'd lived in Yaffo
did not have space between the table and the wall to properly
relax after a meal the way he had been able to do in Plovdiv,
and so he was forced to turn parallel to the table.

Shmuli would not have been Shmuli if he did not sit this way after a meal. Anyone who knew him would say so. His friends constantly pointed it out, laughed about it, would miss it now that he was leaving them and no one was there to turn awkwardly away from the table.

And for Shmuli to sit this way after a meal, be it kebab or falafel or bife de chorizo, his grandparents had to have left Bulgaria for Israel. Yes, yes, his grandparents would have died if they had not left. But the kitchen. The kitchen taught Shmuli's grandfather, Solomon, to sit this way.

And Shmuli's father, Itzhak, watched him do it over and over again—push himself back, lean one elbow on the table, turn his body, and cross his legs. Sometimes he would chew languidly on a toothpick while he did this, and sometimes, tired from his day at work, he would cover his eyes with his hand and briefly nap. But always, he sat this way. For years and years, Shmuli's father watched Solomon and learned the behavior the way children so naturally pick up their parents' quirks. By the time Itzhak was a teenager running around the beaches of Tel Aviv, a surfboard tucked beneath his armpit, he was doing it too.

Either Shmuli picked it up the same way—watching his father do it over and over again—or the repetition worked its way so deep into Itzhak's muscle memory that it reached the genes, reached the DNA itself, and he passed it along to his son so that his son had no chance to resist it.

The first time Shmuli sat the same way, the kitchen in Plovdiv was long forgotten, as were the ones in Yaffo and in Tel Aviv. Now they sat in a dining room in Buenos Aires, where Shmuli, a chubby and happy seven-year-old, adopted another one of the facets of his life that would shape who he was: Spanish.

God, Spanish. Imagine if Shmuli had not crossed the border into Argentina and discovered Spanish. It wasn't so much that Shmuli thought in Spanish, it was that his whole world was colored by it, its sentences flowing like rivers, its sounds the only music Shmuli could move to. Sure, he knew Hebrew. Passably anyway. But to know a language was not to be in that language, not necessarily. And if Shmuli had been raised in Tel Aviv instead of Buenos Aires, he would not have had the language which he loved so dearly that he'd run out at sixteen and gotten it imprinted onto his skin, to his parents' deep chagrin, to the rolling taking place in his grandparents' graves.

Yes, he spoke English too. Well enough that he sometimes made a little money online by writing American kids' essays for them (a racket born out of a slow summer break in January, while kids in the northern hemisphere shivered in their boots on their way to school), well enough that he was on that plane on the way to an American university. But without Spanish, the Shmuli that had come to exist because of mere luck, because of his ancestors' survival, would not truly be Shmuli. He'd be some other kid. One who couldn't reach across the airplane aisle like he was doing now and helping the old lady fill out her customs form.

• • •

Shmuli's parents had lived some extra risk too, but rather than experiencing it while fleeing, they'd chosen to take themselves out of harm's way when they left Israel and its wars. A beautiful place, sure, but why subject children to that? They could take their children away without clamping a hand over their gasping little mouths. They had come from somewhere else, kind of, and felt no loyalty to the land. Appreciation, sure. But the world was wide, and so Itzhak and Dehlia took their two children and their few belongings and they went.

• • •

What a difference the verbs made, Shmuli thought, as the plane touched down. Fleeing, leaving, moving. The world seemed to have very different reactions to each, somehow hating people more the less choice they had.

If you had options and chose the United States, could afford the visas and the tuition, you were the right kind of immigrant. If the only choice you had was to leave or die, to maybe die in the act of leaving, to live a harder life than everyone else in the new country, well, then, you were a scourge.

This was the source of Shmuli's trepidations: a country that would be angered by his existence, by his ancestors' unwillingness to remain in one place. A country that would not understand that the borders his ancestors had crossed were yes, yes, yes, crucial and all that: but they were more than that. They'd made him who he was.

Plenty of people would find his story fascinating and welcome him with open arms. Even those people who were pissed that he'd come wouldn't recognize him, because of the color of his skin, because of his lack of accent, because they couldn't point to one place on the map and say, that, that's the place you should return to.

But they might have hated his grandparents. Huddled on a boat across the Caspian Sea, hidden under blankets across the Syrian Desert. How could Shmuli live in this place with people who might hate his ancestors' survival?

• • •

Anyway, in the history of his family, a crossed border had always been the right move, complicated though it might have been. So Shmuli was looking forward to how this move might change him. How would it add to this unique person who existed unmatched in the world.

He stepped forward in line, his hand clutching his manila envelope of documents, nervous, as if he was getting away with something. He eyed the three agents assigned to his side of the arrival hall, trying to suss out kindness within them. There was a chance, he knew, that they could turn him away. Find him suspicious for one reason or another, despite the visa, despite the envelope. They had that power, though Shmuli knew they were much more likely to use it if his passport said Syria instead of Argentina, if his skin were darker, his English not as good.

Would it always feel like that, in this country? Like he was getting away with something?

• • •

Sixty years earlier, Shmuli's maternal grandmother, Deborah, had felt that way too. Even after her family had left the ma'abara, and the recency of her arrival, or its origin, could not be so easily discovered by the others. Still the feeling seemed to follow her like a stench, like an extra limb grow-

ing from the side of her head, drawing leers. From the camp
to Jerusalem to the kibbutz to Tel Aviv.

"I knew nothing of the journey," she wanted to tell them.
"I know nothing of that other place." They had, most of
them, crossed borders. But it seemed to matter which ones,
and how. She had lived in the camps on the outskirts of the
city, and they had not, so she must have been broken in some
way, less deserving of this place this Jewish diaspora had fled
to (and in doing so had caused others to flee).

The immense flood of people had slowed by then, some
even pouring back out to wherever it was they'd come from,
or to a third place, like Deborah's daughter would eventually
do. The camps had all shut down too, and Deborah knew
that a lot of the feeling was simply that: a feeling. Still, it
felt like she was getting away with something. Like her parents had broken some infallible law of humanity and were
on land that was not meant for them. It was meant for some
other Jewish family, one who'd survived the Holocaust, one
who'd come from a more Jewish place. The right kind of
immigrant, if any.

This might have been why, when Itzhak and Dehlia, years
later, announced they were going to Argentina, Deborah
didn't hesitate to say she would follow them across the world.

●●●

Shmuli stepped forward in line. A little boy who'd probably been awake too long was wailing at his mother's side,
tugging at her hand, yelling that one syllable that children
in almost every language seemed to have deep within them:
"Ma!" Several people, likely as tired and worn down by the

day as the child was, cast dirty glances at the mother, who was attempting to juggle the carriage, her purse, the passports, a half-eaten sleeve of cookies.

He wanted to reach out and offer a hand, though those immigration lines always felt so disapproving, like the rules had all changed and any one of your actions could be punished. Plus, she was at the other end of the line, making it hard for him to simply tuck his manila folder under his arm and provide her with some momentary respite.

It felt wrong not to be able to help, like a cramp or an itch he couldn't scratch, and so he looked away from the mother, scanned the other faces in line. There was something great about the US, how difficult it was to know if someone was local or foreign by appearance alone. Looking at the line for residents, at the foreign line, at the customs agents themselves, it was impossible to distinguish between them with any clarity.

Another step forward, only a few steps away now from officially entering. Weird, too, how you could be in a country but not officially in it until you left a certain part of the airport. What a new thing that was, delineating non-country zones within countries. Shmuli wondered how many more borders had been created since the inception of airports, since the human invention of lines between countries had been blurred by other human inventions.

• • •

In 1941, his paternal grandmother was whisked away from Bulgaria with nothing but what she could hold in her hands. They were small hands, and so she carried little: her pillowcase, her favorite doll, and a saltshaker, because she felt the need to grab just one last thing and it was the only one in sight her hands could hold.

In the future, people would hear this story of fleeing so many times, yet find a way to separate it from the stories that continued. They would forget that the tragedy lay not just in the reason for the fleeing, but in how many succeeded in fleeing only to be turned away. Shmuli's grandparents had not been turned away, and so he existed.

That saltshaker shaped Shmuli, too. Quite literally, because he was ten when he flung it across the room toward his friend, an unfortunate game of catch gone wrong. When he crossed over in his bare feet to the shards littering the floor, one split his toe open. The scar had faded somewhat, but he could still see it curling around the edge of his foot whenever he clipped his toenails. A pinkish white wink, a scythe. It still, to that very day, made him feel a pang of guilt that had far outlasted the pain of the wound itself. He could still see his grandmother's face as she swept the pieces together and gathered them into a plastic bag, which she didn't have the heart to throw out.

She'd died a few years later with the bag still in her bedside table, in the back of the drawer next to her bracelets and passport and the pictures she'd kept of her grandchildren, each one of them a miracle made possible by migration.

• • •

Finally, Shmuli was called forward to an officer. The officer was a black woman who, in his brief amateur observation from the line (not brief enough), seemed to be the friendliest of the officers. He stepped up to the window, set his passport down, the customs form tucked into the page where his visa had been stamped a few weeks earlier.

He said good morning, wondering if his relative lack of accent made him less suspicious or more. She didn't seem to care one way or another and simply asked him for his I-20. He dug his fingers into the envelope, flipping through all the documents he knew he didn't need but his mom had made him bring anyway. In the adjacent line, an officer was speaking heavily accented Spanish at a woman who was struggling to understand. Shmuli wanted to tell her that if she pretended she didn't need this, they'd be more okay with her. But of course he didn't say that, didn't know if the thought had an ounce of truth to it or was just something that was on his mind because of all these things that had shaped him.

His own customs agent typed away, barely looking at him. Then she reached for the I-20 and started to rise from her seat. "Come with me," she said, his passport in her hand. She led him to a room with six or seven rows of chairs all facing a window. There were a handful of people in the room, all looking bored and nervous to varying degrees. Shmuli wanted to rail against this decision to bring him into this room; he wanted to go collect his bag, wanted to make it to his university soon, wanted to enter this new stage of his life. But deep down he'd been expecting something like this all along, and knew that a complaint here would only worsen his mood. It was a luxury his relatives did not have: complaints about waiting rooms.

● ● ●

When they left for Buenos Aires, Dehlia and Itzhak were grilled by friends and relatives about why they would go to a place in such economic disarray. "It's actually turning around for them," they said. "The shekel will go far, and the rockets cannot reach."

"It's been a good year," their friends said, meaning not that many bombings. Meaning: how can you leave home?

"It will continue to be one," Dehlia and Itzhak answered, and raised their glasses.

In Argentina the streets still showed signs of riots, but the glass had been cleaned up and stores were opening, and there was no waiting around for life to come to them. At the synagogue they met Jewish families who had them over for shabbat, though they'd never made it a priority to celebrate back in Israel. Shmuli and his little brother made friends, started rolling their tongues with ease. They played soccer in the streets and the parks, which would make the grassy fields of Shmuli's future university's intramural fields a luxury.

He would become fast and limber, bold in the way he threw himself at the ball on that luxurious grass, not having to fear for scrapes and cuts. A girl on his co-ed team would at first laugh at his movements, then feel a tingle of anticipation before their games, longing to see him again. The temporariness of his visa would cause her anxiety even before they were together, and eventually, when he had to cross a border yet again, she would decide how her life, too, would be shaped by migration.

But that would come later, after he learned to sit parallel

to the table, after Spanish imprinted itself into him, after that little room in which he waited a mere half hour, and, without a hand clamped to his mouth, without anyone hunting him down, without him having to flee, his passport was stamped, and he was waved through into the country.

ABOUT THE AUTHOR

ADI ALSAID is the author of several young adult novels, including *Let's Get Lost*, *Brief Chronicle of Another Stupid Heartbreak*, and *We Didn't Ask for This*. He was born and raised in Mexico City and now lives in Chicago.

SIRSI catalog says
Shelve under:

Alsaid, Adi